PENGUIN BOOKS
THE ROSALES HOUSE

Migs Bravo Dutt is a writer and researcher whose work has been published in several countries, regions, and cultures. Her short fiction has appeared in 22 New Asian Short Stories 2016 and The Best Asian Short Stories 2018. She has co-edited Get Lucky: An Anthology of Philippine and Singapore Writings, a Singapore Writers Festival bestseller in 2015. She has also contributed poetry to various anthologies and journals in Singapore, Asia, Croatia and the USA, and written for Royal Bhutan Druk Air's Tashi Delek and other travel guides and newsletters.

The Rosales House

A Novel

MIGNON BRAVO DUTT

PENGUIN BOOKS

An imprint of Penguin Random House

PENGUIN BOOKS

USA | Canada | UK | Ireland | Australia
New Zealand | India | South Africa | China | Southeast Asia

Penguin Books is part of the Penguin Random House group of companies whose addresses can be found at global.penguinrandomhouse.com

Published by Penguin Random House SEA Pte Ltd
9, Changi South Street 3, Level 08-01,
Singapore 486361

First published in Penguin Books by Penguin Random House SEA 2020

Copyright © Mignon Bravo Dutt 2020

All rights reserved

10 9 8 7 6 5 4 3 2 1

This is a work of fiction. Names, characters, places and incidents are either the product of the author's imagination or are used fictitiously, and any resemblance to any actual person, living or dead, events or locales is entirely coincidental.

ISBN 9789814882125

Typeset in Adobe Caslon Pro by Manipal Technologies Limited, Manipal
Printed at Markono Print Media Pte Ltd, Singapore

This book is sold subject to the condition that it shall not, by way of trade or otherwise, be lent, resold, hired out, or otherwise circulated without the publisher's prior consent in any form of binding or cover other than that in which it is published and without a similar condition including this condition being imposed on the subsequent purchaser.

www.penguin.sg

To Mama, on her 80th birthday

To Bubba and Taatu

1

Singapore

Claire thought of time as a metric that could be rolled out on to a path, one that was unique for each person. Every morning she would run along that imaginary scale where each step was the unit of measurement that took her away from the past and brought her closer to the future. She knew that the future was unforeseeable, however much she ran towards it, yet she would rather race to it than dwell in the past. Many things had happened there, but the past was now immutable and untouchable.

On weekends, like now, Claire would typically go for a longer run. She was on the final stretch near a tennis court when her phone rang. She unclasped the phone from the strap on her sleeve.

'Hello, Claire, hello!' the caller was almost screaming.

'Mama, what is it? Is something wrong?' Claire asked Anna. It was unusual for Anna to call this early.

'Claire, it's about your Lola Gloria,' Anna said.

'What happened to Lola?' Claire asked, her pulse beating faster even though she had already slowed down to a walk.

'She's gone, Claire. She's gone,' cried Anna.

Claire rushed to the nearest stone steps and slumped into the lowest stair without checking if it was damp from the early morning drizzle. She could hear Anna trying to stifle a sob. 'But I talked to her only the other day,' Claire said, holding on to the steel banister by her side.

'She had a terrible slip in the bathroom. We rushed her to the hospital, but it was too late.'

'What did the doctors say?' Claire asked.

'They said it was internal haemorrhage.'

Claire stared at her phone long after the call had ended.

#

At Changi airport, Claire dashed to the Singapore Airlines counter. She skipped the lounge and ran to her gate, almost in a daze, though boarding was still two hours away. On the flight, she stared numbly at the magazines and the *Straits Times*, not bothering to check the in-flight entertainment as she usually did, despite the hundreds of films available. She declined the in-flight meal but opted for a second cup of black coffee, which only made her jittery.

Claire scrolled through the photos she had downloaded on her phone. In each of her milestone photos—from birthdays, graduations, and other celebrations—Gloria was there, beaming beside her, hugging her. Claire had hundreds, or perhaps thousands of photos like these, but even they were not enough to depict Gloria's outsized presence in Claire's life. Claire peered out of the window at the late afternoon clouds. Her Lola Gloria was also there in moments that were too grey to be captured in photographs. It was Gloria who held things together in the aftermath of Claire's broken engagement.

#

Manila

'Ma'am Claire, the van is this way,' greeted Aida, one of her Uncle Ric's helpers. 'Sir JM has also just arrived.' Aida took Claire's black luggage and led her to the vehicle. The driver and the bodyguard were chatting with JM, Claire's cousin, who had also just flown in from Hong Kong.

'I was just talking to her about Christmas plans the other day,' Claire hugged JM tightly.

'It's true when they say nothing could ever prepare us for things like this.' JM gave her a gentle pat on the back.

'We could at least have been by her side,' she said.

'No one could have predicted it would happen this way,' he said.

'I wish there were a faster and safer way to reach home,' she said, shaking her head before going to her seat in the next row.

'From here, it's actually faster to get to another country than to Valle Viejo.' JM pointed at the crawling traffic that greeted them outside the airport. Hawkers were soon knocking on the car windows to sell bottled water and snacks, their increasing presence an indication of the gridlock further ahead.

'I thought you'd be flying with Uncle Ric,' she said.

'Daddy had to go earlier. Besides, I'm scared of flying on those antiquated helicopters that he is fond of borrowing from his friends,' he replied.

Claire's family avoided taking commercial flights to Valle Viejo as they were unreliable and prone to last-minute cancellations. She also feared that the outdated planes would crash in the slightest of turbulence. She would rather bear with this traffic jam.

#

After two hours in gridlock, the van came to its first stop at Ric's home at La Vista, a gated community in Quezon City. Claire brought her carry-on bag with her to the guest bathroom where she freshened up and changed from her skinny jeans and grey jacket into tan slacks and tailored black top.

By the time Claire and JM left the city, it was past midnight. Once the car had exited the expressway gantry and the streetlights became farther apart, JM stretched on his seat, adjusted his neck pillow and dozed off. Claire tried to do the same but kept on waking up at every slight hump.

The long drive felt even more arduous as Claire dreaded each rotation of the wheel that would bring her closer to the end of an era. She tried to mentally roll out her imaginary time scale but could not focus on that either. She was so distraught that all she could conjure up was an image of tangled black ribbons snaking through the mountainous area that the car was passing through. At some point she stopped any more attempts at sleep and simply waited for daybreak. Traffic was still light with hardly any other vehicles except for the occasional jeepneys and tricycles that were overloaded with produce likely bound for markets. But near the mountains, disruption came at closer intervals, as big boulders that had eroded and slipped down blocked parts of the highway, leaving only one passable lane. Here, Claire dared not look out lest she saw a deep ravine, with no guardrail in sight. Then the road zigzagged further up where it was not unusual for faint-hearted travellers to vomit their guts out.

The van stopped in front of a nondescript but clean café on top of the Sierra Madre mountain range. Starbucks could not make it this far, but there were a few local coffee shops like this that had been around for decades now. The café's interior remained unchanged with its wood-panelled walls, round wooden tables, and matching chairs in natural colour. Claire instinctively chose a corner table, Gloria's preferred spot whenever they had made a stopover on their earlier trips together. From here she could look out at the trees below Dalton Pass, the highest point in the Philippines' Cagayan Valley. But, in this cloudy weather, the trees were just dark shadows looming over the valley.

'What's your average these days?' JM asked after Claire had requested for a second cup of coffee.

'Four cups?' she replied.

'Good Lord. You're fully desensitized to caffeine then. I hope it won't come to a point where you'll need it IV-ed into you,' he said. Claire shrugged her shoulders before taking her next sip. 'How's work?' JM knew of her earlier work issues.

'I wish I could say it's going swimmingly. Most of the time I feel as though I'm drowning in workload that goes all the way up to here,' she replied pointing at her neck.

'Same here,' JM sighed. 'Sometimes I wonder why I've chosen this life when I could just be chilling in Valle Viejo.'

'That's the story of our lives,' she said, though in her case, there was at least one reason why she had chosen to stay away from Valle Viejo and the Philippines.

#

Santa Rosa, Valle Viejo

A gigantic stone arch welcomed travellers to Valle Viejo, a province in the northern valley region founded by Spanish priests in the seventeenth century. Claire's hometown, Santa Rosa, nestled in the heart of the valley, was just an hour away.

Santa Rosa's mayor has been a Rosales for several generations. Claire's great-grandfather was the first mayor after World War II, followed by her grandfather. Then it was Ric who had been mayor for almost a decade. After his term, Ric had moved up to the provincial board and ultimately to the congress. Ric's wife, Cecille, had taken over and was the current mayor of Santa Rosa. With each Rosales generation, the clan's influence had only grown stronger: first, with the marriage of Claire's grandfather to Gloria, who came from another prominent political family in the capital city of San Fernando; then, Ric's marriage to Cecille, a niece of a party leader in the region, further augmented the clan's clout.

The longest bridge in the province stood out from its surrounding landscape of green and brown with its orange paint, though peeling in some areas now. This section of the Cagayan River had receded a little since Claire's last visit, making the banks more visible. Perched on a hillside, a church, which was home to the patron saint of travellers, soon came into view. Makeshift kiosks selling candles and religious paraphernalia lined up the roads near the church, where traffic usually slowed down. A gangly boy appeared, hawking candles only to be promptly shooed away by the bodyguard. JM woke up to the sound of a minor scuffle, automatically making the sign of the cross upon realizing he was in front of a church.

An army camp lay a few blocks down from the church. It sat on a vast tract of land fenced in by green sterling wire. Inside was a cluster of white concrete buildings and barracks at a distance from the highway. Then the road diverged, and the car took on the narrower way that led to the town centre. Now there were more houses along the roads. Then, two new churches standing next to each other: the Church of the Latter-day Saints and Kingdom Hall of Jehovah's Witnesses. The car slowed down as the driver navigated the multiple humps near a public primary school. Finally, the car turned left at the end of the stretch and Claire straightened her back when she saw the sign at the corner. They had reached Rosales Street.

Dozens of cars swamped the Rosales compound, which was an entire block fenced in by high concrete walls topped with five layers of barbed wire. The two main gates were wide open today, revealing the chaos inside. People were milling about or huddled in groups under off-white tents that were pitched around the main house—the Rosales House, a name that was given by the townsfolk. Used frequently and widely over time, it had become the unofficial name for the ancestral house of the Rosales clan. More groups of people were sitting on white monobloc chairs that lined up the driveway. When the car stopped, the bodyguard quickly alighted and ushered JM and Claire into the house.

Flowers and wreaths filled the foyer. Ladies in white dresses were praying the rosary near the music alcove; in a corner of the porch, elderly relatives were talking almost in whispers; more people huddled in a row of chairs near the dining hall; and beyond this, helpers were hastily filling trays with beverages and biscuits for the visitors.

A beige carpet, unfamiliar to Claire, covered a patch of the marble floor. A soft glow emanated from a cluster of tall lamps. White flowers. Mass cards were stacked on one side. In the centre was a white coffin. Claire hesitated before moving closer. Gloria looked as though she was merely sleeping peacefully inside the coffin. Claire wanted to believe that Gloria was indeed only sleeping, though she knew it was not so. A light pink rosary was wrapped around Gloria's dainty fingers. This was the same rosary that Pope John Paul II had blessed during one of Gloria's visits to Rome. Claire gently touched the glass top of the coffin. A droplet, perhaps of holy water, that had settled at the edge of the glass cover, caught her eye. Before she knew it, her own tears had merged with the droplet. Not one to show her emotions in public, she gently dabbed the corners of her eyes and bent her head to pray. For a while she had forgotten JM's presence beside her and only realized he was there when he put his arms tenderly around her. They stood there, side by side, united in their grief.

Claire longed to hold her grandmother's hands, but she could only stare at them now. She looked up in an effort to suppress her tears. There were more wreaths around, and from the corner of her eye she could make out the name of the governor across the biggest wreath.

#

'Tita Cecille, where's Daddy and Mama?' Claire asked after hugging Cecille, who was sitting at the receiving line for callers. Claire was half-expecting to see Anna talking to the helpers in the dining area, giving suggestions on how to prepare the food and drinks. Anna was never one to sit still for a long time.

'I've just persuaded them to go rest a bit because they kept vigil all night. Your daddy was just sitting there beside your Lola and wouldn't leave her side even for a few minutes. But early this morning, I managed to convince him to go freshen up,' Cecille said. 'Should I tell the driver to take you home or would you rather wait here?'

'I'll wait upstairs, Tita,' Claire replied. 'I've been meaning to call them, but I couldn't get a signal on my Singapore phone.'

'I've just sent a message to your Mama. She asked me to let her know the minute you get here. Knowing them, they're likely on their way now,' Cecille said.

'Thanks, Tita. I'll be upstairs,' Claire turned to the direction of the staircase.

JM waved at her from across the room and beckoned to her. He was huddled with his friends near the media room, but Claire pointed at the stairs to let him know that she was going up instead.

Claire nodded at the helpers she met on her way up to the room reserved for her, which was adjacent to Gloria's. Maritess, a long-time helper, followed her in not long after. She carried a tray of snacks and drinks that she placed on the coffee table near the picture window. 'Ma'am, you must be hungry after the long drive. Please eat something. I've made you your favourite ham and cheese sandwich,' Maritess said.

'Thank you. I'll have it shortly,' Claire replied.

Maritess suddenly let out a sob. 'Ma'am, your Lola is no longer here with us. What will I do without her? All my life she was here to guide me.' She wiped her eyes with the back of her hand. 'Now I don't know what to do.'

'I'm sorry. I'm sure Lola didn't want to leave you like this.' Claire went over to pat Maritess gently on the shoulder.

'Ma'am, I feel really lost now. I've lived here much longer than I've ever had with my own family. I owe her everything,' she cried.

'I know. It must be very difficult for you, too, but please stop crying now. Here, drink this,' Claire tried to calm her down with a glass of water from the tray.

'I'm sorry, Ma'am, I shouldn't be bothering you with my own worries,' Maritess said.

'Please, Maritess. I understand how you feel. I will talk to Tita Cecille about you,' Claire replied.

'Thank you, Ma'am. Sorry again. I'll go now so that you can rest.'

Claire managed to get a signal and called Dino and Anna, who were indeed on their way to the Rosales House. Though they were mere minutes away from her now, Claire could not wait to be with her parents.

Only a few minutes had passed since Claire came up to the room, but it felt like the clock ticked so much slower. Her mind raced back and forth in time. To her childhood. To times with Gloria who was now gone. To times with Dino and Anna who were still here and had become all the more precious to Claire as she realized how short life could be. She suddenly had this desperate urge to hug them as tight as she could.

Dino was mild mannered. He never raised his voice at anyone, not even at his farm workers when they were at fault. Although he hardly ever spoke out in public, Dino always dispensed the best advice whenever Claire sought his guidance. His steady demeanour always calmed Claire.

Anna was the type who always found something to do, and most of her energy went into caring for the next person. She was the most nurturing member of the Rosales clan, though some who did not know her well enough have perceived this as fussing. Claire grew up not having to ask for things because Anna was always there, anticipating every one of Claire's needs, from her towel to her favourite lunch box. As a kid, Claire also relished bedtime when Anna would share stories about her own childhood, which was clearly from a different milieu. Growing up, Anna did not have many toys and had to improvise a lot by playing with whatever was naturally available to her, like plants, leaves and flowers.

Claire paced around the room to relieve her restlessness. Stacks of magazines were scattered around. They almost seemed structurally built into this house with piles of them in every room. Gloria, the biggest magazine junkie Claire had ever known, had subscribed to several lifestyle and home magazines, both local and international editions. Ric once remarked that if ever the house were to sink, it would definitely be due to the weight of the magazines. Claire picked one up at random and flipped through it aimlessly.

Even without looking, Claire knew the exact moment of Anna's arrival by her Elizabeth Arden Green Tea perfume. Anna was in a long black dress, but without her usual accessories. She hugged Claire tightly, and when she released her, she scrutinised her from every angle as though she had not seen her for ages. 'You've lost weight,' she said.

Claire shook her head. 'It's probably because I'm wearing black, Ma,' Claire explained before going over to hug Dino.

'Did you get any sleep on the drive?' Dino asked Claire as though it was the most important thing in the world. Dino likewise was in a black polo shirt that was neatly tucked into his grey slacks.

'Daddy this must be most difficult for you.' Claire was worried about Dino more than anyone.

'I can't imagine life without her,' Dino said, with a catch in his voice.

'I know, Daddy.' Claire felt her own throat constrict. 'You've been with her every day, and now all of a sudden she's gone,' Claire said.

'I don't even want to think what my days will be like from now on.' Dino stared vacantly at the window curtains.

'I'm relieved that you're here,' Anna told her. 'Your daddy has not slept at all over the past two nights. He can't go on like this.'

'Daddy, I don't have to tell you this. You know this. You have to take care of yourself; more so now than ever,' Claire implored him.

'I'm doing my best,' he said, breathing deeply and exhaling slowly in an effort to calm down. He walked over to the window, drawing the room's heavy old rose-coloured curtains to one side. The room faced the gardens within the compound, usually a peaceful spot, but not tonight. Claire could hear voices. Occasionally an older woman issued loud instructions to a group. The place looked cramped. Even the tennis court beyond the gardens was lined with boxes of ready-to-drink juices and cases of bottled sodas.

Claire saw a group of teenagers in green shirts loitering around. 'Who are they?' she asked, trying to figure out what was written on their uniform.

'Youth volunteers, supporters of your Tita Cecille,' Dino said.

'Why are they wearing those campaign shirts even at the wake?' Claire asked, finally making out the words written on the green shirts: Rosales Forever.

#

Mimi, Gloria's only daughter, arrived from California the next day, heading straight to Gloria's coffin. Dino was at Mimi's side instantly, and they consoled each other amid non-stop sobbing. At times the sobs were punctuated with Mimi's audible cry.

Claire cleared a chair beside her for Mimi. 'Why did she leave us so soon? And why did this happen when I was away?' Mimi said, her voice breaking.

'I've been asking that myself,' Claire said, massaging Mimi's hand gently in an attempt to comfort her.

'I know that death is inevitable, but it should never be this sudden. I didn't even get a chance to say goodbye to Mama properly,' Mimi wept, grabbing a Kleenex box, her nose now clogged and reddish.

#

The next day saw possibly the longest funeral procession in Santa Rosa, with virtually all the townsfolk in attendance. The procession followed the hearse from the Rosales compound all the way to the Roman Catholic church at the other end of the main street. By the time the coffin was laid near the altar, the four-hundred-year-old church was filled up to the last row. People were also standing on either side of the aisle, at the back, and all the way to the church-gate. Claire's family, all wearing white, was ushered into the front pews. The choir started playing a requiem and everybody rose for the ceremony. Then the parish priest, the bishop, the monsignor, and young altar assistants in white habits, walked solemnly to the altar. Claire and JM took turns to read the responsorial psalm from the Bible. She read Psalm 23:4, one of the few passages she remembered and which captured precisely her state of mind—a moment in the darkest valley. After today, she would never see her grandmother again. This mere thought made Claire queasy. It was as though the ground beneath her was shaking. She had to remind herself to deliver the psalm audibly despite her sorrow. She held on to the lectern tighter than necessary.

When the mass ended, members of the family delivered their eulogies. Mimi could barely deliver hers, pausing every now and then as she fought back her tears. Dino was not much better. Only Ric showed restraint.

After the memorial, the funeral procession moved to the town hall for a tribute organized by the local government officials. Mike, JM's younger brother, who was the town's leading council member, closed the segment by thanking the public for their support in this trying time. From there the procession started moving in the direction of the cemetery. Claire, Mimi and Anna, were ushered into a car that tailed the hearse while the male relatives walked with the crowd all the way to the cemetery.

From the family mausoleum on top of a hill, Claire could see the long procession crawling up. It was a sea of hundreds of green umbrellas bearing the Rosales family name—gifts to the supporters during the last election. The scene was not unlike a long motorcade at the height of an electoral campaign, although the mood now was solemn, as was the processional music.

The parish priest officiated another requiem mass at the cemetery just before Claire's grandmother was interred. Claire stayed on at the mausoleum long after the mass until the priest reminded the bereaved family that the funeral service team must now seal the tomb. Claire stepped out and walked carefully past flowers and wreaths to a clear patch that provided a view of the field below the cemetery. Wind-swept corn crops ran parallel to the river, a tributary of the Cagayan River. The sun cast arrows across the water. Soon these would be reduced to shorter darts as morning turned into afternoon. Claire squinted to avoid the sun's glare. Tears flowed but she wiped them off surreptitiously. She raised her face to stem the tears and saw the leaves above her swaying gently. Her grandmother, too, had that kind of an aura, bringing in fresh breeze with her whenever she came into a room. Claire patted away a tiny brown leaf that fell on her white suit-dress and fixed her large-framed sunglasses before joining her family on their way to the waiting cars.

Back at the Rosales compound, chaos resumed as townsfolk jostled for refreshments and pre-packed lunches. But inside the Rosales House, the quietness was almost deafening. Without the flowers and wreaths, the foyer and living room now looked empty. The five-piece brown Italian leather sofa set was back in place, where the coffin lay just a few hours ago. Family members sat around the glass-topped coffee table that was partly covered with trays of mineral water and sodas in cans. Maritess and another helper brought out trays laden with cups of hot coffee and tea.

'We'll need to talk after dinner. I've asked Attorney Corpus to read out Mama's last will and testament in everyone's presence. Dino and Mimi, you must be there,' Ric said standing behind a chair and without making an effort to sit.

'Does it have to be tonight?' Mimi asked.

'There's never a good time to read a last will and testament.' Ric started pacing restlessly behind the longest sofa. 'We might as well get it done at the soonest.'

'But Mama hasn't even settled in her grave.' Mimi's voice was laced with sadness. 'And yet, here we are already talking about how to divide her properties,' she said.

'Ric, Mimi is right,' Dino said. 'We should at least leave it until after the nine-day novena.'

'Look, I know we're all grieving, but the banks will not stop their operations for us. Waiting longer will only complicate the banking transactions and transfers,' Ric said before draining his glass of water. 'Besides, it's better to read the testament while all the three grandchildren are present,' he added, looking at Claire.

That night, Claire drove home with her parents. 'Mama, Daddy, I'm heading back to Manila tomorrow to catch my flight to Singapore on the day after. I'll just go with JM to save the driver an extra trip,' she said.

'Couldn't you stay for a few more days, *hija*?' Anna asked.

'Ma, we have an annual conference next week and I need to be back in Singapore for the presentation dry-runs,' Claire explained.

'But your dad—' Anna said.

'It's okay, Anna. Claire needs to go back,' said Dino, shooting a glance at Claire through the rear-view mirror. 'Don't worry about me, *hija*. Your Auntie Mimi will still be here. She's staying until after Mama's ninth-day novena.'

Claire's room had not changed all that much since her childhood. Her grade school trophies were still neatly arranged in a glass cabinet in one corner. She found it tacky but did not have the heart to tell Anna to put them away. Sometimes she doubted if these trophies were in genuine recognition of her academic performance. Perhaps they had simply been her teachers' way of indulging Gloria. Claire had read *Matilda* in the fourth grade, and she knew that teachers could be mean. She found the extreme, and almost unanimous, niceness of the nuns and teachers at her primary school artificial.

A framed photo of her high school prom was on display on another layer of the shelf along with memorabilia like pins and miniature mugs. For high school, her parents had enrolled Claire in a Catholic school in Manila known for its quality and progressive approach to education. The new campus was twice the size of her former school and had far more students too. Initially Claire had felt lost in the vastness of the campus, but ultimately, she had found comfort in being an ordinary student. She had preferred this status to that of being the cynosure of all eyes back in her primary school.

A charcoal painting of Claire's university graduation picture hung neatly on one side of her room—yet another gift from her grandmother. Like some of her older relatives, Claire had gone to the top state university in the country. Students there had generally scoffed at politicians and their scions, and Claire had been grateful that her parents were not directly into politics and that she was not a congressman's daughter. Claire had never spoken about her political relations, how the Rosales name was almost synonymous with Santa Rosa, and how the family's reach had expanded through the years, boosted by unions with other powerful clans in the region. Only her roommate in the dormitory had known of her connections, but Pia had understood Claire's situation well as she had also come from a similar background. They used to joke about who was wealthier and more powerful, Claire's uncle or Pia's?

'Your uncle owns an entire island and a submarine. He definitely wins this competition hands down,' Claire had often teased Pia.

'Come on, Miss Rosales, what about all those tracts of land that your family owns? And the mansions and houses in Valle Viejo, Quezon City, Baguio, Makati . . . oops, I don't have enough fingers,' Pia had shot back.

#

If it had been up to her, Claire would much rather have been in her room, on her bed, and under her blanket the entire day. She switched off her phone alarm and got up reluctantly. She did not have the energy to do her sun salutations, so she simply sat on her yoga mat, trying to concentrate on her breathing but was swamped with memories of her grandmother. How did other people handle grief? Claire did not have a reference point. She had known despair. She had known misery. But grief—this was new to her. She tried to recall snippets of Joan Didion's *The Year of Magical Thinking*. It talked about grief coming in waves. This, then, was only the beginning for her.

When Claire stepped out of her room, she saw that Anna was with Remy, a long-time help, in the breakfast nook discussing the day's menu. Upon seeing Claire, Remy immediately filled a breakfast tray and brought Claire's cup of coffee, her ham and cheese omelette with two slices of toast, a bowl of tropical fruit, and the daily newspaper. Claire skimmed through the headlines and lifestyle section as Anna and Remy carried on their chatter, breaking off to ask for Claire's opinion every now and then. She was about to fold the paper when she saw Gloria's photograph on a one-page obituary. Claire stared at the face of her grandmother, her hair up in her signature chignon. Gloria looked serene in an off-white *terno o baro at saya*, a traditional Filipiniana blouse and skirt ensemble, made out of pineapple cloth. Claire showed it to Anna, who was surprised to see the obituary and even more surprised to see her own name among the bereaved family members.

'It was probably Uncle Ric's office,' Claire answered Anna's enquiring eyes.

Anna carefully folded the newspaper page neatly and placed it in their glass door cabinet in the drawing room. When Anna came back, she and Remy went about their routine in a way that amused Claire, especially when Remy attempted to make Anna laugh with humorous anecdotes from the kitchen in the 'big house', referring to the Rosales mansion.

Though this house, their family home, was nowhere near as grand as the Rosales House, Claire felt more at peace here. Perhaps the lavender-scented candles that Anna lit every morning radiated harmony. She imagined the delicate scent wafting in all directions, permeating the entire house. The peaceful aura could also be because of the lighter-coloured motif and the wider windows. The pieces of furniture around the house were minimalistic and made of natural materials like rattan and wood, that were complemented by the warm and soothing colours of landscape paintings. In the kitchen, the large window that looked out on to the kitchen garden in the backyard was lined with herbs that Remy used in her cooking. While the décor and scent played a role, Claire knew that the residents' state of mind had a greater impact on the house's overall ambience. Both her parents were usually calm. While they had disagreements every now and then like any other couple, they tended to resolve them peacefully, minus the shouting and drama. If there was anything she could change about her parents, it would be for Dino to be more outspoken in public so that people would learn just how smart he was. As for Anna, Claire sometimes wished for her to start reading more noteworthy books and to get more interested in the arts. Anna always gave her full attention whenever Claire shared stories of her travels, but sometimes she felt Anna was simply indulging her, especially when the topic came to iconic paintings. Anna was not familiar with many of these paintings.

Dino arrived a few minutes later, sitting beside Claire at the breakfast nook. 'If you have time, we can go to Buena Vista for a quick visit,' Dino offered.

'Sure, Daddy, I have a bit of time. I just need to be back by five p.m. as JM will be here to pick me up then,' said Claire. 'And what about you, Mama, aren't you going with us?'

'Your Auntie Beth is coming for lunch, so I need to be home,' Anna replied. 'Dino, I need to tell you something before you go,' she reminded Dino.

Sometimes her parents still puzzled Claire. She was turning thirty soon and yet they still excluded her from some discussions as though she were still a child and they needed to hide grown-up matters from her.

#

On their way to Buena Vista, Claire could see the Rosales's mausoleum towering above the other structures on the cemetery hill, its white cross gleaming on top. She instinctively waved at the direction of her grandmother's tomb. Dino noticed her gesture and smiled. He then pressed the horn as if to let his mother know that they were passing by. The cemetery was located at the highest point of the town as though designed to protect the dead from the floods that the valley had been experiencing more often in the past decade. Soon only the tip of the cross was visible in the mirror on Claire's side as they drove farther down a gentle slope. They reached a junction and turned into a narrower road. They then turned left to a large iron gate, which a young farmer immediately opened. Claire rolled down her car window to soak in the fresh breeze and the greens around her, a rarity back in her urban world.

Buena Vista was at its verdant height. Tall coconut trees lined each side of the long driveway, while mango, paper, and other tropical trees abounded on either side of the lane. Dino drove further up the hill to the centre of the property and parked in front of a white clapboard house. The farmhouse looked exactly the same as Claire remembered it, with its dark green roof and large windows with green-bordered frames. The floor was elevated a few feet from the ground similar to a Gabaldon design, with old brick stone steps leading to a wraparound porch. To the right was a flower garden fenced in white wooden lattice. A small concrete round table with matching chairs and an old swing set remained intact in one corner of the garden. Claire and her cousins used to have their late afternoon snacks at this spot, especially on weekends and summer holidays. As a child, she had felt freer whenever she was here as her parents or grandmother would let her chase dragonflies and butterflies or roll on the grass with her puppy.

Claire was grateful that Dino had inherited the farm knowing his devotion to the property. She alighted from the car and walked to his side. 'Daddy, I wish I had one whole month to stay here—to simply sit on the porch, catch up on my reading, watch the sun sink into the horizon and all,' Claire said, as she lifted her face to savour the breeze and let the wind blow the tips of her layered hair, which had grown a few inches below her shoulders.

'Why don't you apply for a sabbatical?' Dino asked.

'I wish I could, but I'm not yet qualified for one,' she replied.

Dino was soon waving at Ed, the farm manager, who came rushing to meet them.

'Ed, can we go see my trees, the ones I planted with JM and Mike a long, long time ago?' Claire asked on impulse, recalling one of the best times she had with her cousins.

'Ah yes, of course, Ma'am,' he replied.

Claire and Dino followed Ed to the back of the farmhouse, across several seedbeds, and past a wired fence covered with vines that separated the lawn from the tree farm. Ed opened a wicket gate that led to rows of mango trees. The farm's Rottweiler was locked in a fortified doghouse, but upon sensing them, it started barking loudly, inviting more barks from the other dogs. Ed stopped to appease the dog, which quietened down as soon as it recognized him. They then passed by coops of chickens and a special breed of roosters. The latter belonged to Ric, who would sometimes attend cockfight derbies in San Fernando, something that had riled Gloria in the past. They walked past the former cattle barn, which had been converted into storage and garage for tractors when the cattle had been moved to an adjacent pasture. Soon they reached a pond. In a far corner stood about a dozen trees. Claire paused to simply take in this view. She marvelled at how the trees had been spared by the storms and typhoons that perennially plagued this part of the country. When she was in the sixth grade, one of the worst typhoons had struck Valle Viejo and had uprooted hundreds of trees. Buena Vista had suffered a major loss then and Dino had become withdrawn for several months after that storm.

Claire ran towards the first eucalyptus tree in the row. This genus of trees stood out from the rest. While the farmers here cultivated a wide range of trees for fruits or logging, eucalyptus was not one of them, but Claire had been curious to grow one after she had first seen it at a San Fernando suburb. The following week, the plantation owner, who was her grandmother's friend, had sent seedlings and an instruction manual on how to grow eucalyptus.

'It's one of the sturdier varieties, Ma'am,' Ed smiled.

'I can see that,' Claire smiled. 'I remember carving my initials on one of them.'

'Ah, yes, Ma'am. You wrote C-A-R. At first we thought you were trying to spell car, but your Lola had explained that they were your initials. I can't find it now though,' he said.

'Never mind, Ed. That was ages ago. Trees stretch in girth and height, so it's probably lost in the process.' She looked at the hills sloping down the highway, which was virtually empty this time of day, making this area even more tranquil than the other side of Buena Vista.

Claire fell in step with Dino on the walk back. 'What are your plans for the farm, Daddy?' she asked when it was just the two of them.

'I haven't really thought about it. To be honest, I'm not prepared for this. It's different without your Lola,' he replied, his eyes glistening. He looked away and continued to walk, stopping only when they reached a shade.

'Lola wouldn't have entrusted you with such a big responsibility if she didn't believe in you, Daddy,' Claire tried to reassure him.

'It is a huge responsibility. It can be overwhelming, especially when I think about the number of families that depend on the farm,' he said. 'Some of them have been with us for generations,' he added, as he counted the families.

They stopped walking when they heard a car coming up the driveway. 'That must be your Auntie Mimi. She's meeting us at the house,' Dino said.

Claire was used to Dino being silent, but today even Mimi was uncharacteristically quiet at the porch. Perhaps this was how Claire's family grieved. They stopped talking and simply embraced silence. But Claire could not stand the prolonged silence, so she excused herself to go to the toilet even though she did not really need to go. She lingered on the way back to the porch, stopping and checking the decorations that lined the wall as though it was her first time to see them. Then she spotted Dino and Mimi who looked anxious and were now frowning at each other. Claire overheard the last thread of their conversation: 'She has to know sometime. She's mature enough to handle—' Mimi broke off in mid-sentence when Dino signalled Claire's approach.

Mimi put her cup down on the table. She tried to smile at Claire, though her smile looked contrived. 'At what time do you have to leave today?' she asked, though Claire remembered telling her exactly when while they were waiting for their coffee just a few minutes ago.

2

Singapore and Bangkok

Claire started taking a cab to work since her return from Valle Viejo, finding more and more reasons to avoid getting into a bus or the train. It took more effort to smile even at kind strangers these days. In the cab, she avoided any conversation with the driver by putting on her earphones immediately after confirming her destination.

Claire's colleagues extended their perfunctory condolences, but none of them understood her attachment to her grandmother and consequentially, the depth of her grief. Simple tasks suddenly seemed difficult and complex. She found herself struggling to update an Asian business perspective for her advertising company, an easy exercise she had always done efficiently a few times before. She even had a template for this, but now it was taking her twice as long to finish just the first section. She kept changing the colours of her charts, only to revert to the original combination in the end.

If there was anyone among her colleagues who could relate to Claire's current state, it was Marc, a trendy account director, who was sitting beside her on the flight to Bangkok for their company's annual planning session.

'This sounds trite but don't smirk when I say I know exactly how you feel. I've also lost a grandmother, remember?' Marc said.

'I know, you told me. Lola, though, was more than a grandmother to me. She practically made all the major decisions concerning my life, from my birthday celebrations to the choice of my schools,' Claire sighed.

'It sounds like she had an outsized presence in your life,' Marc said.

'Precisely. Even when she wasn't there physically during some occasions, I always had to consider what she would say, how she would react,' Claire said.

'She's left behind a big chasm then. I'm truly sorry,' Marc said. 'My grandmother wasn't as omnipresent, but when my siblings and I were much younger, Grandma used to babysit us while my parents were at work. I don't think my family could have survived without her help.'

'Lola practically provided for all the things that I needed. I'd be nothing without her,' Claire said.

'As I said, it's not the end of the world. Give me your remote, I'll show you something that might help take your mind off your Lola a bit,' he offered, switching to an episode of *30 Rock* in which Jack Donaghy's formidable and strong-willed mother had died and how he imagined her randomly appearing from out of nowhere on several occasions. Claire would have laughed out loud had this been another time, but today she could only manage a superficial chuckle.

Claire used to enjoy shopping in Bangkok, her most frequented city after Manila and Singapore. Here, prices were more reasonable than in Singapore. She would spend hours checking out the various stalls for crafts and curios at the night market in Lumpini Park. In one of her visits one Christmas, she had bought fabric cross-body bags for the kids at Buena Vista and flower-printed sundresses that she had distributed to the farmers' wives. But more than shopping, what had excited her about Bangkok were the vibrant culinary scenes and the avant-garde cafés. She had always looked forward to the authentic Thai iced tea with tapioca pearls and the mango sticky rice at the end of a sumptuous meal. On this trip, though, she declined her colleagues' invitation for after-work drinks partly because she had yet to complete her presentation deck for the next day, but largely because she preferred to be alone.

Back in her room, Claire brought her laptop out, but she was either staring into space or surfing the Internet mindlessly. She switched on the TV, but again found herself flitting from one cable channel to another. She had almost forgotten the pad thai that she had ordered through room service earlier. She nibbled a little, decided it was not to her liking, and pushed the dining trolley out into the hallway. In the darkness of the room, memories of Gloria flooded back clearer than ever. This reminded Claire of the film clips that she used to project on the ceiling as a child. But instead of her favourite fairy tale characters, Claire was mentally replaying images of Gloria on various occasions. When Claire had turned seven, she had received seven special-edition Barbie dolls that Gloria had ordered in advance from the United States so that they would reach in time for her birthday. Gloria was also the one who had given her her first personal computer in high school. When Claire was hospitalized for dengue, Gloria had brought puzzles and a Rubik's cube from Japan to keep Claire busy.

Claire tried to stop the memory flood. This second wave of grief made her sadder than ever. She wished she were back home at Valle Viejo. The pain might have been more bearable if she had been with family. She scanned her brains for book characters who suffered bereavement. How did they handle grief? She remembered Hans Castorp of *The Magic Mountain*, who was orphaned at a much younger age. He was more fortunate in the sense he did not have many memories of his parents that could torture him and make him miss them even more.

Claire had just dozed off when her mobile phone alarm jolted her awake the next day. She went through her morning routine like a zombie. She could not even remember how she got dressed and was in fact surprised that her outfit was coordinated, though to be fair, most of the clothes she had packed for this trip were black with a few grey, white, or tan. She struggled through her presentation and was reading off her PowerPoint slides, which to her would have been tolerable if it were an amateur presenter but not from someone of her position and years of experience. After the day's sessions, Marc and another senior manager, Rinka, practically dragged her to *Cuppa*, a rustic coffee shop tucked in a soi, a tiny alley, off Sukhumvit Road.

'Life has to go on,' Marc advised her in between sips of coffee.

'Easier said than done,' she replied, making an effort to appear more upbeat.

'No, I'm saying it from experience. Not just from Grandma. I hardly talk about this because I still find it painful.' Marc looked at both of them and took a deep breath. 'I've told you about my sister, haven't I? When Mia died in that accident, half of me went with her. It's been years and yet the pain remains. But even the dead would not want you to wallow in sadness for the rest of your life.'

'I didn't know about your sister, Marc,' Rinka shot him a sympathetic look.

'I haven't told many people,' Marc replied. He turned to Claire and said, 'I really wish I had the right words.'

'Thanks, Marc.' Claire closed her eyes and tried to shake off any more memories of Gloria. She did not want to spread her gloom to Marc and Rinka.

'In my belief, death is a natural part of a cycle. Your grandmother's physical body may no longer be here, but she's with you always. Her essence is with you, within you. So, it's not as though you've lost her completely,' Rinka shared. 'As Marc has said, your life has to go on.'

'I'm trying to, believe me. But I'm also feeling guilty that I'm sitting here thousands of miles from my family when we are facing the biggest crisis in our lives,' Claire said. She looked around the café. On other occasions she would have gushed about how lovely it was. It had the perfect mood lights for a rustic ambience. But today, even the coffee tasted too acidic. She stared at the small bubbles until they disappeared, as the coffee grew cold.

3

Santa Rosa, Valle Viejo

Traditionally, the entire Rosales clan attended evening Mass together on Christmas Eve. Then they had *Noche Buena*, the late dinner after Mass, one of the biggest feasts of the year. The highlight of the spread was usually a *lechon*, a whole roasted piglet, placed at the centre of the fourteen-seater dining table. Surrounding it would be stuffed turkeys, *relleno* or stuffed fish, grilled meats and seafood, a huge *queso de bola,* a ball of Edam cheese wrapped in red wax. For dessert, there were layered cakes, native puddings, and other delicacies. After dinner the family would gather around the floor-to-ceiling Christmas tree by the grand staircase. One of the male relatives would mysteriously disappear and return dressed up as Father Christmas to the delight of the kids. Then they would exchange gifts, and by the end of it, the kids would invariably carry more piles of gifts than they could manage.

    This year, Cecille ensured that they had a good spread, similar to the ones in the past. She and the staff replicated the family's traditional annual feast down to the type of queso de bola that everyone was used to. After dinner, Mimi played Christmas carols on the piano and encouraged the rest of the clan to sing along. Ric set about uncorking a bottle of champagne for the ladies and a rare single-malt whisky for the men. Everything seemed to be going smoothly until Dino suddenly started sobbing. He tried to quell it, but his sobbing remained audible. Mimi stopped playing the piano, rushed to Dino's side, and was soon tearing up too. But before the celebration could turn into a cry fest, Cecille gathered JM's and Mike's kids, who were oblivious to the tension in the room, and led them in singing cheerful jingles. Mike also made more effort to be jolly, making funny faces at the kids every now and then. Dino and Mimi eventually calmed down enough for the family to resume their traditional gift-giving ritual.

Breakfast was a subdued affair with the men claiming to have hangovers; and no one bothered with small talk. The silence was broken only when the first carollers arrived at the gate. Cecille excused herself to attend to them. The rest of the family followed suit, suddenly remembering something or other that they had to attend to. All through the morning, hundreds of townsfolk visited, crowding into the compound, to collect their Christmas gifts from the congressman and the mayor. The growing crowd only emphasized Gloria's absence, especially when the elderly ladies expressed how much they missed her.

Dino and Anna headed out early to Buena Vista to prepare for the lunch they were hosting for the farm workers and their families—another tradition that Gloria had instilled. Claire and the other relatives followed them to the farm later that morning. The biggest barn was cleared and decorated for the occasion. About fifteen white round tables covered in red tablecloths formed a U facing the makeshift stage, which had a big MERRY CHRISTMAS banner on the wall. On one side of the barn, caterers served buffet food to the guests. Those who were not yet in the queue, especially the kids, were jumping around and dancing to lively music. Ed went up to the mic and announced the start of the programme, requesting Dino to join him onstage. Dino opened the event with a short speech; initially ill at ease with this new role, but his sincerity took over and elicited warm cheers from the crowd. Ed called out prizes for the grown-ups and encouraged more singing and dancing. Mimi also announced that she would be handing out additional prizes to the dancers and musicians, inviting more cheers.

Claire played with some of the kids, fascinated at how noisily the little ones slurped their spaghetti. She would never forget their unadulterated joy at seeing the surprises in their loot bags that were filled with toys and sweets. Claire looked up at the stage and could not help but notice how truly happy Dino and Anna were handing out presents to the farmers. She had never seen them in charge of family events before, or seen Dino speak in public, even if that public consisted only of farmers and their families. Anna herself was a revelation—she had managed to maintain the traditional feast and had even added new features to this year's party—ice sculptures and a bell-shaped piñata that was a huge hit with the kids. The buffet lunch was also above Claire's expectations. She raised her chin as she waved at Dino and Anna onstage. Even she was beginning to feel the joy of Christmas.

Claire stayed on at the farm after the party. From her seat on a white rattan sofa on the north-facing section of the porch, she could see the rolling hills and the hundreds of cattle grazing on the adjacent pasture. Beyond lay the centuries-old cathedral, its spires glinting in the late afternoon sun. The rays that streamed through the screen from the other side of the porch added more glitter to the string of silver and gold balls wrapped around a Christmas tree in the corner. She gently dusted one of the green-and-white cushions that blended with the rest of the farmhouse's decor. The wooden square coffee table held more Christmas emblems, including a potted poinsettia in full bloom and a pair of red scented candles in glittery hurricane lamps. She was about to pick up one of the candles when she noticed Dino approaching.

'Congrats, Daddy. That was a great party. You and Mama did an outstanding job,' Claire hugged Dino.

'Thanks. Your Mama did much of the work as usual. She's still there at the barn with Lorna, preparing food packs for the families who could not attend the party,' Dino replied.

'I'm truly impressed. I've never seen you and Mama so engaged.' Claire's remark made Dino self-conscious, his cheeks almost matching the pale red of his checked polo shirt. He awkwardly ran his fingers over his hair, now greying in areas. Claire changed the topic, 'What's the plan for New Year's Eve?'

'Countdown at the big house as usual,' Dino smiled. 'And for New Year's Day, your Auntie Mimi has booked us into a new spa resort near San Fernando. You can have your massage, and your mum and I can go for a dip in the pool for a change.'

#

The sky above the Rosales House was ablaze with colourful fireworks on New Year's Eve. Kids were blowing their trumpets loudly, adding to the noise. Mimi held the mallet of a large gong at the centre of the courtyard and the young kids jumped every time she struck the gong; this was the same ritual that Claire, JM and Mike followed when they were kids, believing, too, that jumping to the sound of the gong would help them grow faster in the new year.

At the spa the next day, Claire luxuriated in the deep tissue massage that the manager had recommended. She was lulled to sleep by the fragrance of the scented candles lined on a *sungka* piece and the soothing yoga music playing softly in the background. She found comfort in being with her family and the fact that the family survived this first holiday season without Gloria. A deep chasm still remained that only time could bridge. Waves of sadness still came back every now and then but they ceased to be the onslaught they were earlier. The waves did not slam, but rather came at gentle intervals, bringing in sweet memories of Gloria each time.

On the drive back home, Claire closed her eyes and reclined on the backseat relishing the days of togetherness. Times like these were rare now, especially for someone like her who lived by herself in another country. These were the sweet moments she had traded off for the order that the city-state was known for.

She felt rejuvenated by the collective energy of her family, despite their scars and all.

Upon reaching home, Anna excused herself to change out of her damp clothes while Claire and Dino went straight to the family room. Dino looked around, trying to decide what to do next.

'No music tonight, Daddy?' Claire asked. Dino would normally play soothing music when they spent time together.

'I can put something on if you want,' Dino replied.

'No, there's no need,' she shook her head. 'I was just wondering why you didn't automatically switch your turntable on.'

'You're very perceptive as usual, *hija*. In fact, I wanted to talk to you about something before you leave for Singapore,' he said.

'What is it about?' she asked.

'Now, as in tonight, is not the best time to talk about it. I need your Auntie Mimi to be around. Let's have some music after all.' He went over to put on a collection of classical piano music. Soon Claude Debussy's *Clair de Lune* filled the room.

'Ah, this is going to send me off to sleep straightaway,' Claire said, reclining on her favourite cane armchair.

'It was Mama's favourite,' Dino smiled at the memory.

'And now, ours too,' she said.

'It was Mama who suggested that we named you Claire. We all know where her inspiration came from.' Dino loved to repeat this story about Gloria's favourite piano piece.

Anna, having changed into her sleepwear and a pink floral robe, strode in with a glass of warm milk. She religiously followed her doctor's advice to drink milk before bed to address her calcium deficiency. Remy followed her in with a tray of herbal tea for Dino and Claire.

'Did you have fun at the spa? Was it up to your standards?' Anna asked, coming to sit on the side of the sofa near Claire's armchair. It was on this spot and on relaxing nights like this when Anna would share stories about Anna's childhood.

'Of course, Mama. I even dozed off during my massage,' Claire said.

'That's the best indication that it's effective,' Dino chuckled. 'We all know how you fight sleep off. You've been doing it ever since you were a child.'

Claire smiled before sipping her tea but could not wait to be alone in her room. This was the first time that Dino had asked to have a serious talk with her, and she had no clue what it was about. She needed to do her breathing exercise to reduce the anxiety that had started to build up.

#

Buena Vista

At Buena Vista the next day, Dino asked Lorna to serve their breakfast at Claire's favourite spot on the porch. Despite the familiar surroundings, which had invariably comforted her in the past, Claire's feeling of dread remained unabated. Claire, who had not been praying regularly since high school, found herself doing so fervently. She was mentally hoping that any revelation would not drastically change things with her family.

Mimi tried to smile, but it looked forced. Mimi then attempted to talk about the next holidays.

Claire tried to relish her sunny side-up, garlic fried-rice, dried milkfish, and *longganisa*, a type of pork sausage from Vigan in Ilocos Sur. Having an elaborate breakfast like this was a rare luxury for her, who did not have time for breakfast on a regular day in Singapore. At any other time, she would be savouring this moment. Instead, here she was, anxious and still trying to second-guess the reason for this meeting.

Lorna came to refill their coffee cups and clear their plates. After she had left and was out of earshot, Mimi and Dino sent each other non-verbal signals, as if nudging the other to start the conversation already. It was Mimi who ultimately broke the uncomfortable silence. '*Hija*, we need to talk to you about something very important. But first, know that our strength as a clan comes from our unity. We will always be the solid Rosales clan as long as we are united. Nothing should come between us. And remember, too, that we all love you dearly.'

'Auntie, you're making me nervous.' Claire tried to take calming breaths.

'This confession is long overdue. But, as your Auntie Mimi has just said, whatever you learn from us today should not change things between us,' Dino said, speaking more deliberately as though in a foreign language.

'Daddy, please just say what you have to say. Don't keep me in suspense.' Claire knew this talk took a lot of effort for someone naturally reserved like Dino. His unusual preamble had already set off alarm bells, and Claire had a feeling his revelation would turn her world upside down despite all his assurances. Her stomach started grumbling despite the breakfast she just had.

'You meant the whole world to your Lola and she did everything in her power to keep you from hurt and harm. But there is a secret that she kept from everyone outside of our immediate family,' Dino continued.

'Daddy, just say it,' Claire said, her throat drying all of a sudden.

Dino took a deep breath before coming over to Claire. He held her hands tightly. 'Claire, *hija*, I am not your biological father,' he said, almost in a whisper.

'What are you saying, Daddy?' Claire exclaimed, standing up and shaking Dino's hands off.

'I may not be your biological father, but I've always regarded you as my very own daughter,' he added regaining his breath and hugging her. Claire extricated herself and started to pace around the porch.

'Claire, I've never doubted your daddy's dedication to you from day one,' Mimi said. 'You could not find a better father than Dino. You are very blessed to have him.'

'I'm very fortunate to have Daddy, there was never any doubt about that. But who is my biological father? And why has he given me up?' she asked incredulously.

'It's your uncle Ric,' Mimi replied almost inaudibly.

'How did that happen?' Claire asked hysterically. 'And why are you telling me all this only now? After thirty years!'

Dino asked her to lower her voice lest the helpers got alarmed. 'It's a long story,' he sighed.

'How could you stay quiet all these years?' she demanded, looking at Dino and Mimi like they were criminals.

'Claire, you know the business our family is in. Your Lola made us promise to keep this a secret out of fear that it would damage the Rosales clan,' Dino whispered.

The three had to pause when Lorna came back with more fresh fruits for dessert. Mimi told Lorna that they did not want to be disturbed from hereon.

'Damage? I could damage this venerable clan?' Claire asked sarcastically.

'Your Lola did not want Ric to lose his chance at mayoralty back then. Cecille had an influential uncle who had promised to help Ric win the election—the first one for Ric,' Mimi explained.

'So, you all tried to hide my existence so he could win that goddamn election?' Claire could not help but raise an eyebrow.

'At that time, your Lola and we thought it was for the best,' Dino said.

'And why didn't you come clean after he had won the election? Why wait all these years?' Claire demanded.

'I had my own motives. Having experienced what it was like to have you in our lives, your Mama and I wanted to keep things as they were,' Dino said.

'What about my biological mother? Who is she?' Claire pressed on, now angry with everyone—her grandmother, Ric and all her family members. They—all of them—had betrayed her.

'I am sorry, Claire, but I don't have much information about her. She was a student at the time, and that's all I know. Mama probably paid her off to be quiet,' said Mimi, taking out an envelope from her purse and handing it to Claire. 'This has some information about her.'

Claire looked at the envelope but didn't have the courage to open it. 'Who else knows about this? Does Auntie Cecille also know?' she asked, pointing at the envelope.

'To my knowledge, she knows that you are not Dino and Anna's biological daughter, but she doesn't know about Ric's involvement in this. I'm not sure if that has changed,' Mimi said.

'Does everyone in town know that I'm adopted? Is that why people stare at me curiously whenever we're at those public events?' Claire felt as though her chest was about to explode. She inhaled deeply and mustered all her strength to stop the onset of tears. 'A fish in an aquarium, there for all to see.'

'Claire, don't say such things. Nobody knows about this outside of the family,' Mimi got up from her chair and stopped Claire from pacing around.

'But why didn't you tell me this earlier?' Claire wiped off her tears before turning around to face Dino and Mimi.

'You know how we always had to defer to Mama for most, if not all, major decisions,' Dino said trying to calm her down. 'Call me a coward, but I didn't want this revelation to come between us. We were trying to protect what we have. You.'

#

When they had returned to their family house from their trip to Buena Vista, Claire went straight to her room and uncharacteristically locked her door. She was shaking with anger now and was cursing everyone under her breath, even kicking the wardrobe door in frustration. She did not want to open the brown envelope yet and slipped it into the zippered pocket of her suitcase instead.

Anna knocked on her door. Claire initially ignored her but was forced to open the door when the knocks became louder.

'Claire, are you okay, *anak ko*?' asked Anna. My child. Anna would call her this whenever Anna felt that Claire was in distress and needed comforting.

'I'm okay, Mama. I'm just making sure that I'm not forgetting anything,' she pointed at the pile of things on the bed.

'You must know we love you very much. We are always here for you no matter what,' Anna said.

'I know that, Mama. I'm grateful to you and Daddy for everything,' she replied.

'Nothing should change,' Anna said tentatively.

'I understand,' she said, but did not elaborate. She hugged Anna tighter than ever, which somewhat surprised Anna.

Mimi came to her room next and asked Claire if she needed more information.

'Why does it sound as if Daddy and Mama immediately agreed to adopt me? Isn't parenthood an immense decision? Didn't they want a family of their own?' Claire asked as she put her packing cubes and foldable toiletry bag into her suitcase.

'Dino is medically incapable of having a child. He very much wanted to start his own family immediately after his marriage and so he was completely devastated when he found out he couldn't have children. You came at the right time for him and Anna, an answer to their prayers,' Mimi explained.

'And Mama? What's her story?' Claire sighed.

'Don't you know about their elopement?' Mimi seemed surprised. Dino, at the time a research trainee at an agrochemical company, had feared that Gloria would not allow him to marry Anna, who hailed from a less-privileged family in the South, who had yet to finish college. They had gotten married secretly at city hall.

'I've heard bits and pieces from various people. But how could Mama keep THIS a secret?' she asked pointing at herself.

'That only goes to show how dedicated she is to you and Dino. To the best of my knowledge, Anna doesn't know of Ric's role in this.'

'Yes, we must not forget about Uncle Ric,' Claire could not help rolling her eyes. 'Shouldn't I be talking to Uncle Ric about this? After all he was the one who started the fire. And shouldn't Tita Cecille know the truth? What other stories did Lola make up to hide the truth about my existence? I should have known she was capable of keeping many secrets ever since she had told me that sun and moon story. A tale of secrets, she had said.'

'Claire, your Lola may not have been perfect, but also remember that she has done many things for you. Let her rest in her grave now,' Mimi said. 'Please don't bring this up to Ric or Cecille for now,' she begged.

'Why not? They're both grown-ups. Why hide things from them?' Claire snapped.

'I hate to tell you this, but Ric and Cecille are facing marital issues,' Mimi sighed for what seemed like the nth time this morning.

'Look, out of respect for you and Daddy, I'll be quiet for now. But unlike you, I can't keep a secret forever. The truth must come out . . . and it must come out sooner,' she closed her suitcase with more force than required.

4

Singapore

Singapore hosted an inordinate number of runs–like bank-sponsored ones, various charity runs, fun runs, as well as the dawn, sundown, and night marathons. Claire had her first charity run during her first year in the city-state when her company had sponsored one for UNICEF. She had thought the event was 'just for fun' and had signed up without any prior training. She soon found out that it was a ten-kilometre run. The next day, she had woken up with severe aches and pains, and had almost had to crawl to her bus stop, a hundred metres away from her place. She realized, however, that running was emotionally rewarding. She had, since then, collected finisher medals in several marathons. Regardless of the run, she found gratification in completing the race, more than in competing against the other runners.

It was also because of running that she and Pia had reconnected, after bumping into each other at a charity run to benefit the typhoon victims of the Philippines. Since then, she and Pia had run several marathons together.

Running at Singapore's Bedok Reservoir helped Claire calm her mind. She usually came here with Pia, but on this day, she decided to come on her own. Now, more than at any other time, she was grateful for the tranquillity of the park. On weekdays like today, the park was almost empty, which was possibly why it had become an alarmingly popular suicide point.

But this afternoon, she ignored eerie thoughts as she listened to her playlist, which started with Coldplay songs, followed by her David Guetta mix, and an EDM mix that she had bought from Collette, a concept store in Paris. She slowed down as she approached her finish line and walked to a nearby bench. She watched the sun's reflection on the gleaming lake, the ray shining on a lone kayaker sailing across the waters to the other side, leaving tiny ripples in his wake. Then other kayakers arrived, pulling boats out of the docks, and racing amid splashes and cheers.

Claire got up from the bench and strolled over to a narrow boardwalk on the other side of the park. Her thoughts drifted to that point two weeks ago when she finally had the courage to take out the envelope that Mimi had handed her. Seated on her bed, she tore the top flap of the envelope and unfolded the three-page document.

Melanie Delfin Montero. That was the name written in bold at the top of the first page. It was the name of her biological mother. Alone in her room, Claire had read the name aloud several times. Montero, Montero. It had sounded strange. She had said it out loud a few more times and it still sounded like a faraway country. Claire had been researching about Melanie Montero for the past two weeks now. She had checked Google, Facebook, and LinkedIn, which had churned out more than thirty potential Melanie Monteros. She did not know if Melanie Montero had retained this surname or if she had changed it after her marriage—whether she was married at all. With the help of a private investigator, Claire narrowed her search down to six potentials. Three were in Latin American countries, two in the United States, and one in Italy. Initially she found it strange that no one from the Philippines turned up during her search, but she did not discount the last six—Filipinos could be found even in the farthest corners of the world. Her tribe was the modern-day nomads. In all her years of travel, it was not unusual to hear a Tagalog-speaking person within a ten-metre radius, be it in Paris, New York, London, or even in a small village in Luxembourg.

The Melanie Montero in Italy was an exchange student from Mexico while the one in Florida was a young mother, younger than Claire. The other Melanie Montero, now Smith, was based in New York, and fit the profile that Claire was looking for. Claire temporarily updated her LinkedIn profile to reflect her Andres middle name, as seeing the Rosales surname could make the real Melanie suspicious. Some of her friends immediately reacted upon seeing the change, despite her muting the profile changes; but they accepted her explanation that it was for a short experiment at work. After a few days, Claire mustered enough courage to send an email to the New York-based Melanie. She introduced herself as someone from the same university, the University of the Philippines, also known by its acronym, UP. Claire asked permission from Melanie Montero Smith to network, seeing they might have a few things in common. She emphasized, however, that Melanie should not feel pressured or obliged to do so.

A loud splash from the reservoir brought Claire's gaze back to the kayakers, a group of employees doing team building activities, who had just returned to the dock. They waved their flags in victory and shared jubilant shouts. She yearned for the day when she too could shout jubilantly, or at least regain her baseline equilibrium. But she was grateful that gradually her sadness had become more bearable and was no longer the heavy burden she had been carrying around for a long time. The waves of grief felt more like mere ripples now.

Claire took out her water bottle. It was probably unusually humid, as she felt thirsty even after draining the bottle. She bought another bottle from a nearby vending machine. On her way back to her bench, she watched young mothers with prams strolling in and congregating by an ice cream stand, letting their babies babble at each other. An old man started doing a martial arts routine as kids around him chased each other.

Out of habit, Claire checked her emails—the coming months would be busy with travels, including a trip to New York. In her work, Claire had done several analyses and released a few white papers on the skincare category that her company appointed her a strategy expert for. This also meant working with several project teams in various regions, sometimes for weeks on end without any breaks, and with many of the days stretching well into the nights too. This was the first time that she was going to work with the team in North America on a big project, and if they won this project, it would be a career breakthrough for her, too. All these, though, became secondary to what had been preoccupying her just now— the prospect of meeting her biological mother in New York.

5

New York

The coffee shop at Claire's hotel was less crowded than most cafés in the Manhattan area off Fifth Avenue. It was conducive for a meeting that had the potential of becoming emotional. She arrived fifteen minutes early and chose a table by the window facing Madison Avenue. On the way to her table, she picked up a copy of the *New York Times* from a neat row of papers by the window. She paused for a few minutes to take in the view of the crossroads below. Unlike other days, there were fewer yellow cabs coming into the area as most of the offices were closed for the weekend. She was skimming through the paper when a woman, slightly taller than her five-foot-five stature, approached her.

'You must be Claire?' asked the woman, in a soft, but clear and confident voice. She was wearing a black turtleneck top over a pair of dark grey jeans, and a belted jacket that she removed and folded neatly before draping over the back of her chair. Her clothes were not figure hugging, but fit her appropriately given her age, which seemed to be early fifties.

'Yes, I am,' she replied, standing up and offering to shake Melanie's hands. Claire learned that Melanie worked as a psychotherapist at Bellevue Hospital. 'What's the most interesting case you've handled?' she asked.

'Way too many. Most recently, there was this ex-banker who seemed so put together, always in his business suit, but who's mentally stuck in the nineties. He lost all memories of his life after the nineties because he could not cope with the reality after that period. His career failed. His marriage failed. He lost his home. He realized he didn't have as many friends as he had thought. I get depressed thinking about it now.'

'I'm sorry. We can talk about something else,' Claire said.

'Many stories like that just show us how frail human nature is. Some people could look put together on the outside, but deep down they could be a mess. Anyway, let's talk about your career instead. It does sound more interesting to me,' Melanie smiled. They talked about each other's work as though they were strangers who just happened to sit beside each other during a long-haul flight.

After their coffee was served, Melanie straightened her back. 'I know why you looked me up,' she said. 'I had half-expected you to do that when you turned eighteen. I was somewhat disappointed that it did not happen then. After that, my hope simply dimmed with the years. This, happening now, is a bit of a surprise after all these years.'

'I only learned about it recently, after Lola Gloria passed away,' Claire said.

'I'm sorry to hear about your grandmother,' Melanie replied.

'Thank you,' Claire said. She didn't want to say anything more about Gloria.

'I also did my own research about you. I must say you've accomplished a lot at your age, and I somehow feel a sense of pride in that,' she smiled trying to look unruffled, although she was fidgeting and her hands were shaking mildly.

'My parents are the kindest people I know, and they have taken care of me in the best way possible. Perhaps that's why it never occurred to me that they weren't my biological parents. Of course, my grandmother was always there, with her generous gifts and all. But now I suspect that her actions were more out of guilt than love,' Claire said, shaking her head as she pushed her angry thoughts at Gloria to the back of her mind. For now.

Melanie looked out of the window, in part to avoid Claire's gaze. She gave a soft but deep sigh before looking at Claire again, her eyes now shimmering. 'You must think I am heartless. I can't blame you if you detest me,' she said.

'Before this meeting, I didn't have much of you to think about.'

'Fair enough,' she replied.

'But what I really want to know, and have been dying to ask you is this: why have you given me up?' asked Claire, trying her best to sound detached.

'Please understand that it happened when I was very young,' Melanie held her coffee cup tightly. 'My story is not very unusual. I came from a poor family in Cebu and I got into UP on a scholarship. I met Ricardo at a conference that my organization hosted. At the time, Ricardo was an aide of an influential lawmaker, I guess as part of his training as an up-and-coming politician,' she paused to take a small sip of her coffee. 'After the session, he invited me to dinner. Then he started showing up after my class. I was taken by his sophistication and superficial charm,' she added.

'Didn't you know that he was married?' Claire asked.

'I was quite naïve. It never occurred to me that he was. I just assumed that everyone had pure intentions as I had.'

'When you found out that you were pregnant, I'm sure you were smart enough to know that you could have . . . you know . . .' Claire could not bring herself to say the word.

'It occurred to me, but I couldn't live with that choice. I told Ricardo that I would have the baby no matter what. It was only then that he told me he was married and that, if his wife were to find out, it would be the end of his political career even before it began,' said Melanie.

'And?' Claire prompted. She did not want Melanie to stop. She wanted the entire truth laid out once and for all.

'He introduced me to your grandmother the next day, in a discreet restaurant on Tomas Morato Avenue. Your grandmother, as you must know very well, was a force. She told me to think of my parents. I wasn't sure if she had known about my background and economic situation before that, but her words hit me hard. I couldn't disappoint my parents and the entire village that was rooting for me. I was probably the first from our village who would be completing a degree from the country's most prestigious university.' Melanie looked downcast.

Melanie was soft-spoken, the type who would not use foul and vulgar language, but could speak forcefully if required. It would be easy to like her as a colleague, an older relative, or a best friend's mother, but it was difficult for Claire to reconcile this Melanie sitting before her with a woman who gave up her own daughter. This, to her, was possibly the biggest form of rejection for a human being, even worse than abortion. Claire tried to imagine herself in Melanie's shoes, but however hard she tried, she could not see herself forsaking her own child out of filial duty. 'Out of curiosity, how did you manage to hide your pregnancy from other people, especially during the last trimester?' Claire asked.

'My close friends were as naïve as I was. They did not notice the changes in my body at the time. I wasn't showing until the sixth month, and when I started to show, I told my friends it was a side-effect of a steroidal medicine I had been taking. Then I simply hid from everyone in my last trimester. It was more manageable then. Remember this was before Internet and mobile phones,' Melanie said.

'But what about your parents?' Claire asked.

'I told them I was doing an internship at a provincial hospital so I could not spend the school break back home. My parents didn't ask too many questions. It was easier to lie to them than to my friends,' Melanie said the last sentence in a much sadder tone.

'How did you give birth? I'm sorry to ask you all these questions, but nobody bothered to give me the details of how I came into this world,' said Claire, reminding herself to pretend she was interviewing a random person on the street, not someone who had carried her in her womb for nine months.

'Your grandmother took me to Laguna. She rented a room near San Pedro and she paid the landlord's wife to look after me.

She knew a doctor who owned a small hospital nearby. Your adoptive parents were called over immediately after I had given birth. It was Dino's kindness that made me agree to the adoption,' Melanie said.

'In all these, that's one thing I'm truly grateful for, having Daddy for a father,' Claire said.

'Someone from city hall came immediately and asked Dino and Anna to sign the papers and subsequently file your birth certificate. So, technically, you are not legally adopted as, from birth, Dino and Anna were registered as your parents,' said Melanie, her voice quavering.

'That's why it never occurred to me that I was adopted. My birth certificate has them as my parents. I've always thought of them as my parents. And perhaps it was indeed for the best,' Claire tried to keep a lid on her thoughts but could not hold this one.

'Your grandmother promised to help me finish college, but only if I signed a document relinquishing any claim on you and not to be anywhere near you. It read like a permanent restraining order actually. She asked me to sign it while I was still dazed from the anaesthesia.'

Claire wanted to ask if Melanie had ever held her in her arms, or looked at her before she handed her to Dino and Anna. She wanted to ask if Melanie had even checked whether she had ten fingers and ten toes. She wanted to know whether baby Claire had cried loudly or had merely whimpered. But all that was immaterial now. It would not change the past. Claire bit her lip as she waited for Melanie to continue.

'I did my graduate studies and applied for a research grant that brought me here. Then I found a job that kept me here.' Melanie was now looking drained. She ordered a second cup of coffee and suggested that they meet again the next day so that she could take Claire to the Museum of Modern Art or the Metropolitan Museum of Art.

Claire saw Melanie off to the hotel exit by the Madison Avenue side. They hugged each other under the hotel signage, but Claire was conscious not to keep it too tight or too long such that to a casual observer it would look as though they were mere acquaintances who had bumped into each other, a scene that was not unusual in this bustling city. Melanie then crossed the street, turning once to wave at Claire.

Late that afternoon, Claire went for a run in Central Park. It was a sunny spring day but still cold by Claire's standards even though she was wearing a running jacket. She ran as fast as she could, oblivious to the crowd along the way, determined to beat her record both in time and distance. Claire ran past one of the big ponds and stopped by a bench to catch her breath. Nearby, a street artist was sketching the portrait of a middle-aged man, the latter seemingly forced into it by his eager wife who paid for this memento. Claire absent-mindedly followed the artist's quick strokes. She imagined Ric in a similar sketch but immediately cleared her head of this mental caricature. She could never be proud of Ric. How could a father be so indifferent to his own daughter? Was he like this to his sons also? She tried to recall occasions when Ric was with JM and Mike, and the only times that came to mind were during Christmas gatherings. Even then, she could not remember Ric jesting around with his sons, who were more likely to play with their bodyguards.

On her walk back to the hotel, Claire passed by a young mother pushing a pram. Every now and then the mother would stop to check and show her face to her baby, who babbled enthusiastically as they played peek-a-boo. Claire remembered Melanie. Was Melanie any better than Ric in the morality department? Melanie seemed highly intelligent and in many ways more accomplished than most women Claire knew. But, in a way, Melanie was also not too different from a mercenary.

#

Claire and Melanie had been touring the Museum of Modern Art for an hour when they reached Van Gogh's *Starry Night*. Here Claire saw the psychologist in Melanie when she talked about the pain that haunted Van Gogh and how each stroke in this masterpiece could be an expression of anguish. This piece of art, which had the power to give pleasure to hundreds or thousands of aficionados, might have been a receptacle for an artist's pain. It could contain hundreds of hours of heartache.

While walking around the museum, Melanie told Claire about her two children. Nate, the eldest, was in his final year at a Boston university, while Melissa was a sophomore in California. Claire could not help but ask if they knew about her existence.

'No, they don't know about you yet. My husband and I decided we should not torture them with something that was hypothetical until yesterday,' Melanie replied. Apparently, her husband had known about the whole story even prior to their marriage twenty-five years ago.

'Does your husband know about our meeting now?' asked Claire.

'Yes. In fact, he wanted to meet you, but I felt it was rather too soon. You might not have been comfortable with the idea.'

After the museum, Claire saw Melanie off near the subway at 57th Street. Claire told Melanie she would be returning with a friend for the New York marathon, a bucket-list item.

'We should meet again then. Let me know closer to the date,' Melanie said before hugging her, somewhat tighter than the previous time. 'Please take care,' she said before heading towards the subway entrance.

Claire retraced her steps back to Fifth Avenue and walked aimlessly around until she realized she was in front of Saint Patrick's Cathedral. As though on autopilot, Claire went inside, dropped a coin in the collection box, and lit a candle. She chose a pew near the altar and found solace in the church. After a while, she lit another candle. She watched the flame from the other candles dance. Sometimes the flames flared with the opening of a door but would eventually flicker gently. The newly lit ones gave off thicker smoke, and Claire followed the path of the one she had just lit. It was as though the dread she had been carrying with her for some time now had eased up, evaporating with the candle's smoke.

Back at Fifth Avenue, Claire suddenly felt the impulse of skipping like a happy child, even kicking some cigarette butts out of the way, something that she would normally cringe at doing. But conscious that people might think her odd, she pinched her arm to remind herself that she was all grown-up and should behave like one. She briskly tried to blend in with the New York pedestrians. She stopped by Barnes & Noble and picked up a couple of books on her list. Seeing that she still had time, she went upstairs, ordered a cup of coffee, sat at a small table facing the Philippines Embassy, and browsed through the dailies. Even the front-page looked more optimistic that day: there was no bombing in Iraq or Afghanistan, nor any airline explosion, or tsunami, earthquake, or deluge in other parts of the world. The first quarter financial reports were out, and while the US economy had not yet fully recovered, the Federal Reserve had predicted stability by year end. The worst was almost over and prospects were brightening for the world in general.

Near her hotel, she stopped to read the quotes along the path leading to the New York Public Library and tried to memorize Kate Chopin's: 'The bird that would soar above the level plain of tradition and prejudice must have strong wings.'

6

Singapore

Varying degrees of illumination had always enthralled Claire. Today, she got up earlier than usual, which she blamed on jetlag. She stepped out on to her balcony and watched as dawn gave way to daylight. Sometimes she would sit here with her camera and wait for the blue hour in the morning and sometimes it would take her hours to capture a single moment of sunrise. Today, though, she simply wanted to sit and savour the moment.

Claire was beginning to like the idea of having a mother with whom she could talk at a more cerebral level. She started comparing Anna to Melanie. While Anna always tried her best, Claire could not talk to her freely about her angst, her thoughts, or her deepest passions. Moreover, Anna was not fond of museums. Anna knew about *Mona Lisa* because of a Nat King Cole song and of Van Gogh's *Starry Night*, again because of a popular folk song, but she was not aware of other critically-acclaimed paintings. At times, Claire wished that she could also talk to Anna about her favourite literary fiction books or at least one of Jane Austen's, but Anna hardly read and had very few books in her shelf. The few she owned were by Barbara Cartland and other authors in that genre. Once Claire had gifted her a Jane Austen collection for Christmas; but, Anna was yet to read them.

Anna liked handbags and purses with big logos. A huge contrast to Melanie's understated elegance.

But why was Claire overcritical of Anna and why was she comparing her to Melanie? She closed her eyes to clear her mind. To be fair, bags and purses were Anna's sole weakness. Anna was never extravagant on other things. Anna once mentioned that carrying the right purse helped make her feel that she truly belonged, especially when surrounded by the other Rosales women. Those logos helped reduce her insecurity.

#

On her way to the office the next day Claire decided to pick up coffee first to shake off her jetlag and its attendant thoughts. She ran into Marc at the basement coffee shop.

'How was your trip?' Marc asked while waiting for their coffee.

'The usual drill. Working late and on weekends and practically working like a zombie twenty-four hours before the submission.'

'Boring,' Marc said, rolling his eyes. 'Met someone interesting?'

'Office people as usual. You might know some of them. What about the places, don't you want to know about the cool, trendy spots?' she said.

'Well, you know me, I'm more interested in people than places,' he smirked. 'Besides I think I know you. You probably went to, at most, three places . . . other than the office and your hotel. Hmmm, let me guess . . . which were the three places you visited? Could they be a coffee shop, a bookstore, and a museum? Wait. Are they three different places?' Marc continued on their way to the office.

'How could you be right as always even on a Monday morning? Yes, I've been to all three places. I found a coffee shop in a bookstore and another in a museum, but have yet to see all three in one space,' she said. They continued their banter all the way to the lift.

'My sixth sense tells me the boss is here and is not looking happy,' Marc whispered as they reached their office lobby.

'What's going on?' Claire whispered back.

'Apparently there's another shake-up at the top. It shouldn't affect us. I'll tell you at lunch,' Marc said, waving before vanishing to his wing.

#

'What's up with Chris?' Claire asked as soon as they got a table at a bistro in their office tower. Chris was their regional managing director.

'Haven't you heard the latest yet?' Marc said, in between sips of Coke Zero.

'How would I know? I've been away for more weeks than I can remember.'

'I've forgotten that you spend more time outside than in the office. Anyway, according to Marie, Chris is going through a rough patch.'

'What kind of rough patch? And how would Marie know?'

'Of course Marie would know; she sees all the emails to and from Chris. Apparently, Chris is not hitting his targets,' Marc whispered. 'My little mole told me that he might be reassigned, or possibly worse.'

'What does that mean for us?'

'I don't think it would impact us directly. You're not reporting to him a hundred per cent, are you? In any case, he's facing P&L issues. And luckily those aren't in our KPIs.'

'True that. But in his current mood, Chris makes the office gloomy. As it is, we have far more work than hours in any given day.'

'We'll survive. Just remember how many CEOs have come and gone since you've joined this company,' Marc said.

#

Claire avoided the office as much as she could and scheduled most of her client meetings outside the office. It was after one of these off-site meetings that she managed to catch up with Pia at a café on Orchard Road. It seemed not so long ago that Claire and Pia had bumped into each other at East Coast Park at the charity run for the typhoon victims. Since then, they had been hanging out on weekends and sometimes meeting up for dinner on weekdays as well. If Claire did not feel homesick at times, it was largely due to Pia who made her feel as if they were still in the Philippines and not living in another country. Pia always knew where to find the latest Filipino restaurant in the city. It was as though she had a special power and could immediately smell it if anything new was cooking.

Pia also kept Claire updated about the Filipino community in Singapore. Pia actively participated in the Philippine Embassy's cultural programs and in their university alumni association events. Claire, on the other hand, had a more erratic schedule due to business travels that she stopped being active in either circle. Even back in university, Pia had been the more outgoing of the two, and kept trying, but failed, to recruit Claire to her Greek sorority, which was known for their various social activities. Claire had gravitated to academic and cause-oriented organizations. Claire had felt so strongly about unfair tuition-fee hikes and some government policies that she had joined rallies and demonstrations against these. She had written wall news about the real state of the nation, but eventually had to tone it down when the dormitory administration threatened to inform her parents about her political activities. They would not renew her stay if she would be seen in anti-government rallies again unless she had parental consent, they said, and she knew that getting one would be next to impossible.

Counselling each other on office matters was a regular part of Claire and Pia's catch-up. They would commiserate about the difficulty of navigating a diverse environment and working with colleagues from different cultures. While everyone did the utmost to be polite and cooperative, it was not unusual to have miscommunication now and then because of language and cultural differences. Claire consciously tried to be more flexible to suit her client's requirements. This seemed to work for her as clients occasionally gave her positive feedback. One such email was even shared around by their Human

Resources Director as an example of outstanding client service. Meanwhile, Pia tended to be more assertive, having been trained as a lawyer in the Philippines' top law school. She had been terribly unhappy in her two previous companies that every time they met, Pia had one complaint or another, but now she was happier, in her current job at a pharmaceutical company. It was Claire who was having work problems this time around.

'How do you deal with a grumpy manager?' Claire asked.

'Wait, wait, wait. I'm not used to you grumbling like this,' Pia commented.

'I'm really bothered by the atmosphere in the office,' Claire said.

'You've been in the company for long, I'm sure you can outlast your manager,' Pia said.

'The thing is, Chris is not usually this aloof or toxic. Perhaps it's the latest pressures on him making him behave this way,' she said.

'Could be. In that case, try to detach. Have a life outside of the office,' Pia said. 'You should come with me next Wednesday. Dinner at the Ambassador's residence.'

'What do you get out of those, anyway?' she asked.

'You get to meet some of our kababayans,' Pia replied, referring to their fellow Filipinos.

'I don't have the time. As it is, I hardly see you on some weeks,' she said.

7

Singapore

The following weekend, Claire and Pia went for their run in the Botanic Gardens. This time, they planned a longer route starting by the Bukit Timah Gate and ending at the Tanglin Gate, as suggested by their fitness trainer in preparation for the New York City marathon. They had been training more intensely for two months now, running twice on weekdays and covering longer distances on weekends to build their endurance. Today, Claire, was running slower than Pia, so she told her to go ahead and just meet her at the café later for breakfast. She slowed down to catch her breath near a lily pond and then stopped to watch the fish cluster around the breadcrumbs a toddler had thrown at them. She reluctantly resumed her run and jogged to the visitor centre, where Pia was stretched out on one of the chairs. Claire was into her cooling-down exercises when suddenly everything around her started to swirl. Then she blacked out. The next thing she knew, she was sprawled on the pavement and seemed to have twisted her ankle. Pia called for help. A middle-aged couple rushed to her side and the man immediately called a cab while Pia and the lady helped Claire up. Together, with her arms around their shoulders, they helped her into the cab. Pia then took Claire to the Gleneagles hospital despite Claire's protest.

'Your pulse rate, blood pressure, and temperature are now normal. We'll do an ECG to help us understand better what caused the syncope. As for your ankle, we'll do an X-ray to check for any fracture,' the A&E doctor explained to her.

Claire looked at her swollen ankle for the first time and realized that she could not put back her running shoe on anymore. By now the pain was so excruciating that she immediately took the ibuprofen the nurse gave her. She looked at her ankle again and it dawned on her that she might not be able to run the NYC marathon, which was just a few weeks away.

'Don't think about it now. First, we must find out why you passed out,' Pia said.

Another nurse arrived with a wheelchair and ushered Claire out of the A&E and into the hospital's main ward.

'I'll follow you to your room. I'll just get something to drink from the cafeteria,' Pia said before the nurse and Claire got into the lift.

Soon, Claire was wheeled down a corridor and into her room. 'The doctor will come in the afternoon to read the test results,' the nurse said. She raised Claire's leg and rested it on a cushion. 'Keep your leg in this position while I go and get the icepack,' she added.

Pia returned with her coffee and went to sit by the window. 'I'll sit with you for a couple of hours.' She started leafing through a magazine.

'Thanks, but there really is no need,' Claire said. She closed her eyes not so much because of the pain, but because of her growing frustration with the forced immobility. She was also starting to get impatient with the wait for the diagnosis. Then her phone rang.

'Claire, what happened to you? Pia said you were rushed to the hospital.' It was Anna, in a high-pitched voice.

'Ma, it's nothing serious. I've merely twisted my ankle. That's all. They're keeping me only for observation, but I should be discharged by this evening or tomorrow,' she explained.

'Claire, I'm going there immediately. You can't be in the hospital by yourself.'

'Mama, it's nothing. I should be up and about in a day.'

'No, I am on my way Claire. Your daddy has already called our travel agent to book the flights.'

Claire sighed after the call. She shook her head as she looked at Pia.

'What? I panicked, okay? You lost consciousness all of a sudden, for God's sake,' Pia explained.

'Thanks. It's just that I don't want them to fuss. You know how they are.'

'It's not fussing. Come on, you're their only Rosales princess. I can't just leave you alone like that,' Pia replied.

'Dear Lord, Pia. You're exaggerating.' Claire winced as she felt the excruciating pain in her leg. It had been more than four hours since she had taken the pain reliever; perhaps its effect had worn off.

Soon after, Claire's phone rang again. It was Mimi this time. Claire went through the same dialogue she had had with Anna.

Claire had taken a nap after Pia had left and woke up only when the nurse brought in her lunch. She did not have an appetite but ate a portion of the congee and steamed fish anyway, realizing that she had only had the fruit bar Pia had forced her to eat. She was about to switch on the TV, when the nurse opened the door and ushered in Marc and Rinka.

'Claire, what happened?' Marc rushed to her side.

'I tripped and twisted my ankle,' Claire said pointing to her bandaged leg.

'But Pia said you had syncope. What the hell is "syncope", anyway?' he asked.

'Pia really pulled a telethon today,' she said.

'I'm glad Pia was with you when it happened,' Rinka chimed in. 'Here, I've Googled "syncope",' she said passing her phone to Marc. 'But why would you lose consciousness all of a sudden, Claire? What did the doctors say?'

'They haven't said anything yet. You know how doctors here are. They want to see all the test results before drawing a conclusion. I'll get the results only this evening,' she explained.

Marc and Rinka still looked puzzled, so Claire rolled her eyes in mocked annoyance. 'I know what both of you are thinking. Before you waste any more time, let me nullify that first hypothesis. I'm not pregnant, okay?' she said.

'Really? That's sad. I was hoping you were, Claire; you're not getting any younger,' Marc joked.

'Am I missing something here? If she were pregnant, who's the lucky guy?' Rinka asked.

'That's precisely the point. If I were, it would only be the second case of parthenogenesis ever,' she added.

'Well, I wouldn't be surprised if God had decided to choose you as Mother Mary 2.0 given your unassailable virtues,' Marc winked at her.

The visit became an occasion for the three to talk about Chris and the office situation, so it was almost dusk before they realized it. The nurse came and advised Claire that the doctor would visit her any time now. Rinka excused herself to meet some friends for dinner, while Marc stepped out to buy coffee from Tanglin Mall. After a few minutes, the doctor arrived and said, 'I have some good news and some not-so-good news for you, Miss Rosales. The good news is, your ECG is normal. And the not-so-good news, your haemoglobin count is below the normal range. This puts you at risk of anaemia. You have to start taking vitamin B12 and iron supplements.'

'Thank you. So does that mean I can go home now?' Claire asked.

'Not so fast,' the doctor said, pointing to her ankle. He pulled out the X-ray result and showed her the fracture in her ankle. 'We have to do the surgery tomorrow,' the doctor added, before summoning the nurse to give her further instructions. 'But don't worry, if all goes well, you can be discharged the next day,' he informed Claire before leaving.

Marc came back with Claire's favourite pasta take-away from Café Beviamo. After setting up their dinner, he switched the TV on and settled on the HGTV channel. After a while, he switched it to *How I Met Your Mother*. He was so engrossed in the show, that he only stirred from the couch when the hospital PA announced the end of visiting hour.

'All right, that's the hospital kicking me out. I'll be back tomorrow, after breakfast. Or, if you like, I could come in earlier with some proper breakfast for you,' he offered.

'After breakfast is fine. I can survive a day of hospital food. It's not so bad,' she said.

'If you say so. Call me any time, even if you need me in the night.' He kissed her on the forehead before leaving.

#

Anna reached the hospital around lunchtime the next day. She had left Valle Viejo immediately upon learning about Claire's condition and had gone straight to the airport for the first flight to Singapore.

'We've all been so worried,' she said, when she reached Claire's bedside. 'Can we call your daddy? He wanted to come too, but had to stay back because of some issues on the farm,' Anna added.

Claire called Dino to assure him that she was well, and then passed the phone to Anna, who, after updating him about Claire, was now recounting the details of her trip—it was the first time Anna had travelled overseas by herself, and there was pride in her voice as she narrated this experience to Dino. She went to Claire's bedside after the call and was again checking Claire's bandaged ankle looking at it longer than necessary.

'Mama, it's nothing serious. But I'm glad that you came,' Claire said.

Anna's arrival was timely. She saw Claire before she was wheeled in for surgery. Anna waited right outside the operation theatre, even though the doctor said she could stay in the ward.

It was a quick procedure that was completed in less than two hours. Because of the anaesthesia, Claire did not feel any pain, though she could feel the incision being made.

'Ma, you didn't have to wait there all this time,' Claire said on the way back to the ward.

'Oh no, that would have made me even more restless,' she said.

Once back in the room, Anna drank water and heaved a deep sigh of relief.

'Now that you know I'm okay, you might as well go out for some shopping. Tanglin Mall is just down the road,' Claire smiled.

'Indeed, I've not shopped in a long time. We've been rather busy at the farm because of this El Niño. It hasn't rained in a long time. It's the worst weather in years. Most farmers are already writing off the season as a total loss—they don't expect to harvest anything,' Anna replied.

'Is it that bad? Now I feel worse that you're not with Daddy at this time,' she said.

'He was more worried about you,' Anna replied. 'But now that I'm here to take care of you, he can focus on the farm,' she added.

Claire fared better the next day, although her ankle was still swaddled in a heavy cast. Marc checked her out of the hospital and took both her and Anna home. By now Claire had accepted that the NYC marathon was a no go.

Claire urged Anna to go out for some shopping, not wanting her to be cooped up indoors as she hardly visited Singapore anyway. 'Ma, please. I am not sick in any real sense, okay. You can go out. I can get by for a few hours on my own,' she said.

'Oh, please. I love shopping, but it can wait. I'm here to take care of you before anything else.'

When Claire could not persuade Anna, she called in Dino to help her change her mother's mind. Anna finally gave in, but said she would be out for only three hours at the most. 'Do I look okay in this dress?' she asked. She was wearing a long, printed, wrap-around dress with a matching thin belt.

'Of course, Mama. You always look fabulous,' Claire smiled.

'Thanks. I can never be too sure living in the province and all.' She looked doubtfully at her reflection in the full-length mirror.

'Mama, clothes don't make a person,' Claire sighed.

'Ah, if only I had the confidence of the Rosales women.' She lifted her chin and straightened her back.

'But you're a Rosales woman yourself,' Claire said.

'Only by affiliation,' she replied.

'You've been one long enough,' Claire reassured her.

'Ah, but I could never forget the fact that at one point I had to borrow my cousin's old dress for my high school graduation,' Anna shook her head at the memory.

'Ma, you never told me this before,' Claire exclaimed. Although Anna had shared stories about her childhood, Claire never thought her situation to have been this dire.

'You'll never understand, Claire. You have no idea what poor people are like, how they live. Never mind. It's not your lot,' she smiled. 'See you later, *hija*,' she kissed her on the way out.

Nowadays, Claire listened intently whenever Anna told her about her past. She had learned more about Anna in the last year or so, since Claire discovered the circumstances surrounding her birth. She had also become more curious about Anna while she was learning more about Melanie. Claire had begun seeing Anna in a new light with each new revelation. Anna was not the shallow person she had assumed she was. She was a fighter and a survivor, and she never forgot where she came from. She always found ways to help the less fortunate.

Claire picked up an old book that she loved to read over and over again. Marcel Proust's *Swann's Way* comforted her in more ways than one. She loved to imagine the paths young Marcel and his parents would frequent on their post-dinner walks in Combray. She savoured each and every sentence and could memorize the passage about madeleines and how they had stirred childhood memories for Marcel. But this time, Claire started feeling restless after just a few minutes of reading. She picked up her phone and checked her mails, something she felt self-conscious to do in Anna's presence. She saw an email from Melanie asking about the NYC marathon, so Claire replied, explaining what had happened. Melanie rang up immediately after. She sounded different on the call and was not as calm as Claire remembered her to be.

'Are you sure it's minor, or are you just making it sound like that?' Melanie asked for the second time.

'As I said, it's nothing serious. Otherwise, I would still be in the hospital,' Claire said.

'Fair enough. But, how come the doctor couldn't explain the reason for your fainting?' Melanie insisted.

'It's an unusual case, Melanie, but I'm not patient zero either. There were precedents. In my case, though, it was exacerbated by micronutrient deficiency,' Claire said.

In the afternoon, Anna came back in a happier frame of mind carrying two shopping bags. She excitedly unwrapped a Gucci tote she had purchased at a discount.

'Mama, this was from last season,' Claire explained.

'Who cares, as long as it has this logo,' Anna pointed at the interlinked Gs. 'In Valle Viejo, more so in Santa Rosa, nobody cares whether it's last season's or this season's. What's important is the brand name,' she added. She tried on the bag and walked around the drawing room.

'Who are you wearing?' Claire mimicked Hollywood presenters of fashion shows.

'Oh please indulge me once in a while,' she said coming to sit beside her.

'I've never stopped you from doing anything. Ma, if there's anything else you want to buy, you can use my card,' Claire offered.

'Oh thanks. But I have a supplementary card from your daddy. I should stop buying all this stuff though,' Anna said.

'You haven't bought much . . . just a couple of items,' Claire pointed out.

'I know. It's just that I feel guilty when I see the price. I can afford it now being a Rosales and all, but every now and then I remember how hard it was for me as a child.' Anna looked saddened by this memory.

'Oh, Ma, that was a long time ago. And this is now. As I've said, you've been a Rosales for the most part of your life,' Claire hugged Anna.

'Can you imagine, I didn't even have a proper doll when I was growing up. In fact, I was just as excited as you were, probably more, when you got those special edition Barbies from your Lola,' Anna sighed.

'Mama, I feel really bad that you had a tough childhood. But I'm so proud of you for having the strength to overcome it and put all that behind you. Daddy and I are truly blessed to have you,' Claire rested her head on Anna's shoulder.

'Oh, *hija*, you're making me cry now,' Anna said, wiping her tears away.

Claire, too, was teary eyed but hid this from Anna. She felt warm and fuzzy and would have wanted to hug Anna a bit longer if Anna had not started tearing up.

Marc dropped in with coffee after office. 'I'm sure you're dying to have your favourite brew,' he said, as he took out the coffee from the paper bag and placed it on the glass-topped table. 'I've also got something for your mum,' he said, bringing out another cup.

'Thanks, I've been craving for a good brew all day!' Claire was genuinely glad to have her flat white for the first time after so many days.

'There's an extra charge for delivery,' Marc replied.

'Yeah, right,' she pretended to roll her eyes.

Anna had her coffee with them, but then excused herself after a few minutes to resume her dinner preparation.

Marc brought out some DVDs including *Mad Men*, a TV series that Claire was not really fond of, but which Marc urged her to watch. 'Watch the first season before you make up your mind. TV is different nowadays. It's the new cinema actually. I mean, nothing is happening on the big screen apart from those superhero sequels or remakes. The real breakthroughs are in TV,' he said.

'How do you know all this?'

'My brother, Josh, is an industry-insider. He's a screenwriter. So, yes, this point of view is from an expert panellist. Any more questions?' he raised an eyebrow.

'Wow, you're so lucky to have family who're in-the-know,' she stared at Marc in amazement.

'You should meet Josh. He's quite an insightful guy. Not just about showbiz. He actually hates the showbiz people. The irony,' he said.

#

Two weeks later, Claire's orthopaedician removed the cast on her leg. However, she still had to use her crutches for another week. In any case, she felt relieved to see the bandage go.

True to her word, Anna returned to the Philippines only when she was assured that Claire was on the mend. As soon as she was back in Valle Viejo, Anna messaged Claire regularly using her new iPhone—she and Dino were amused with the new purchase, particularly its touchscreen feature.

Sometimes Claire had reason to believe that there was, indeed, a time and reason for everything. She had more time to talk with her parents now and felt as though the distance between them had reduced in the process.

JM came to Singapore for work-related meetings the following Monday. After office, he arrived at Claire's place, carrying dinner take-aways. He set up their so-called TV dinner, placing Claire's *kway teow* on the side-table closest to her, before settling down on the adjacent chair.

'What are you having?' Claire asked.

'I've missed having chicken rice, so it was the first thing I ordered,' he replied, showing her the two orders of chicken rice on his tray.

'Why am I not surprised that you've ordered chicken rice for two people?' Claire smiled.

'You know me too well,' he grinned between bites of the food.

'How are the folks back home?' she asked.

'Same old, same old, for the oldies, I guess,' JM replied. 'As for the next-in-lines, I'm excited about Mike. He really has a strong chance of making it in next year's election.' Mike was the only one in their generation of Rosaleses who had returned to Valle Viejo after university to carry on the so-called 'family tradition'.

'He should. I don't know much about his rivals but based on what Daddy had told me, Mike is by far the most qualified.'

'True that. The other candidates are utterly incompetent. Mike deserves to have his turn,' JM replied.

'I agree. 110 per cent. Will you be home during the campaign period then?'

'Of course. I've already applied for a two-week annual leave.'

'I'm excited for him, but I'm not sure I'd be able to go home in May,' she said.

'You were never one to join the fray anyway. We'd be more worried about you if you got on to the campaign trail,' JM teased her.

'You mean to say I'm more of an impediment, incapable of swinging any votes and all?'

'Well, there's that. And of course, there's your security, the most precious Rosales heiress,' JM added.

'You're no different from Pia. You make me sound as though I were a crowned princess of a very rich kingdom. Anyways, what about Uncle Ric, what's his game plan?' she asked.

'I don't really know about Daddy. I don't talk to him that much. I suppose he would run for re-election. What else would he do?' JM replied.

'Is anyone challenging him this time around?'

'There are rumours.'

'Who would dare oppose him?' Claire was surprised.

'In politics there are always opportunists, as they say. Some intelligence bit points to a potentially nasty fight come May. I don't know all the details yet and am clueless at the moment, but Mummy said we should be prepared for the worst,' JM explained.

'This sounds scarier than I expected,' Claire frowned.

'Yeah, that's why you too should be prepared to go home. Who knows, your one vote might make a difference,' JM said.

Claire dreaded that it could actually happen. She wanted to ask more about Ric but did not want to put the burden on JM who probably didn't have a clue about Claire's current struggles.

JM practically followed the same routine the rest of the week, dropping by at Claire's after work and bringing dinner each time. He would fetch and carry things for her and forbade her from moving around. He even ran her errands and restocked her fridge with fruits and basic grocery items like milk, cheese, and bread. On JM's last night in the city, Claire insisted that she take him out to dinner. 'Come on, it's high time you meet other people and see other places,' she urged.

'Okay, fine,' he nodded. 'But please, I don't want you to go to too much trouble. Let's go somewhere where you don't need to walk much.'

'Then let's go to Prego. Do you remember the place from your last visit? You devoured the mozzarella and heirloom tomatoes there in, like, five seconds,' she said.

'Of course, I remember it, but I also love anything labelled FOOD, as I'm sure you know. You weren't surprised when I'd ordered two servings of chicken rice,' he laughed at the memory.

'I'm an early witness to your talent for inhaling food. Even when as a kid you'd always order two burgers at McDonald's or Jollibee,' she joined JM in his laughter.

'Ah well, those were the good ol' days. Now I need to be more disciplined or I'll end up with a cardiovascular disease,' JM said.

'That's true. We're not getting any younger. Anyway, your big appetite doesn't show . . . yet,' she added.

'Thanks to my new and improved gym trainer,' he flexed the muscles in his right bicep as he mimicked the booming voice-overs from old TV commercials.

'By the way, is it okay if I also invite Marc to dinner?' she asked.

'Of course, I'd love to see him again,' he replied.

'Let me call him then,' she said, reaching for her mobile phone on the coffee table. 'He said his brother was in town, but would love to meet up, if we're cool with that?'

'The more the merrier,' JM raised both thumbs.

Claire felt like an old lady with the way JM held her arm on the way to the restaurant. He still did not let her go even when she told him she was capable of walking with the help of her crutches. She heaved a sigh of relief when she saw Marc and his brother approaching. With two other people around, JM would stop being overly solicitous and she could enjoy dinner in peace.

'And this is my much older brother, Josh, who looks much younger than me,' Marc said when it was his turn to introduce Josh.

'I'm actually just a couple of years older, but way older in emotional maturity,' Josh smiled as he shook JM's and Claire's hands.

'It looks like there's so much brotherly love in the air,' JM joined in the banter.

'Kidding aside, I love Marc to bits, that's why I've come all the way for a family hug,' Josh added.

'That is so sweet,' Claire said.

Contrary to Claire's expectations, the dinner was far from quiet. Both JM and Marc were TV and movie buffs and they didn't seem to run out of things to talk about. The affair almost felt like a game of movie charades as both loved to play out the most memorable scenes as well. Josh stepped in whenever arbitration was required between the two—they clearly deferred to his expertise.

'It's too early to call it a night,' JM commented after they had paid the bill.

'Why don't we go check out the rooftop bar?' Marc suggested.

'I didn't know there was one in this building. What say you?' JM asked Claire.

'Well, if you guys don't mind my crutches,' Claire smiled, 'I'm more than happy to be in your gracious company.'

'With three gentlemen by your side, there's no better time to be in crutches,' Josh smiled.

'Well said, Josh,' JM said.

They took the lift to the seventieth floor and JM was immediately awestruck with the iconic view from this height. They were led to a corner table with an unimpeded view of the city. JM basked in the glow of the nightlights, clearly enjoying the scene. Claire looked at Marc and sent him a grateful nod.

'You should have told me to bring my camera,' JM told Claire. They both shared photography as a hobby, although JM preferred to take architectural photos and night shots while Claire favoured nature and macro pictures.

'How could I have known that we'd end up all the way up here, me in crutches and all,' she said.

'You should have told me to bring my camera,' JM repeated, but this time to Marc.

'Well, how could I have known that I'd get invited to an impromptu dinner,' Marc replied. 'Josh did you bring that compact but powerful camera of yours?'

'Now that you mention it,' Josh said, taking a few shots. 'I'll email them to all of you,' he said before asking JM and Claire to write their email addresses on a table napkin. 'Get well soon, Claire. I'll email you an interesting article on hacking the NYC Marathon,' he said.

It was way past midnight when JM dropped Claire off at her apartment. After the lively atmosphere at the bar, Claire now started feeling sad to see JM go.

'Claire, I'm just a phone call away,' he said, helping her to the sofa.

'I wish we all lived in the same city and closer to each other. We could get together more often and more easily,' she wiped small tears that gathered at the corners of her eyes.

'That's one thing I've always wished for, too. We are such a small clan and yet we are so widely dispersed geographically. I live in another city. Auntie Mimi lives in yet another one and even farther at that.'

'And all of us hardly visit Valle Viejo, a place that feels so far away, both in distance and milieu,' she said.

'Precisely. But don't worry. I will call soon and more often. So stop crying and be the brave girl you always claim to be,' he kissed her forehead before walking to the door.

Although she generally hated being fussed over, Claire found the extra attention from her family and close relatives heart-warming. She smiled to herself as she recalled how Anna and JM had taken care of her during their respective visits. She also enjoyed getting more calls from Mimi during her medical leave. She was not immune to extra TLC after all.

#

A couple of days later, Claire was surprised to get a new caller in Josh. 'Hi Claire, I got your number from Marc. He mentioned that you're still on medical leave. I thought I'd check if I could be of help or if you're dying of boredom. Maybe you could come down for a coffee. We could go to a café near your place?' he asked. 'Phew, sorry if I said all that in one go,' he added.

'Hi Josh, good to hear from you. Indeed, I could do with some coffee,' she said, suddenly excited that she would not be sitting at home all day today.

Josh picked Claire up from her condo's lobby and helped her into a cab. The nearest café was *Toast Box*, a local coffee chain known for its Nanyang coffee and *kaya* toast. Though it was only a few blocks away, Josh had insisted that she should not walk and had called a cab.

'Thanks for accepting my invitation. Marc was supposed to spend the day with me but was pulled into an urgent meeting after lunch. I didn't want to be that aimless guy wasting his day at tourist central,' he said.

'Glad to be of help. What brings you to Singapore, I mean, aside from visiting Marc?' Claire asked.

'I had a meeting with a studio in Kuala Lumpur. Then I decided to swing by for a couple of days to visit Marc. We haven't seen each other for almost a year now, can you imagine?' he said.

'That's a long time. Marc must be so happy that you're here,' she said. 'Wait, I think our order is ready,' Claire added seeing that their order badge was buzzing.

'Oh, yeah . . . I'll go get it,' he said picking up the buzzer and going to the counter. He returned to their table with a tray laden with two cups of coffee and a plate of kaya toasts. 'This looks healthy, doesn't it?' he pointed at the butter.

'Very healthy indeed. So go easy on that,' she suggested.

'Why would I? Life is too short as they say,' he smiled. 'Hmmm, this coffee smells good. What is it called? Kopi O?' he asked.

'Yep, it's black coffee basically,' Claire replied.

'But you said something else when we ordered,' Josh said.

'Oh, I said Kopi O Kosong. Kosong means nothing. That is, no sugar,' she explained.

'Kopi O Kosong. Kool with a K. You're making my day,' he grinned before taking a sip. 'So what do you do in your downtime?' he asked.

'I'm a boring person. When I'm not running, I'm reading. Or vice versa,' she answered.

'What do you like to read?' he leaned forward to listen.

'Are you interviewing me for an article or something?' she smiled.

'Okay, fine. Let's talk about the weather then,' he laughed.

'Oh no. That's a dead-end street. There are only two types of weather here as the locals would say: With Aircon and Without Aircon. Anyway, going back to books. I like to read literary fiction from everywhere. Not just from the US or the UK. Some of my favourite stories are actually translations. I love Halldór Laxness for example. And you?' she asked.

'I like American literature. Faulkner, Fitzgerald, naturally. And also French. Proust, Flaubert, and all. But also Modiano,' he said.

Before she knew it, Claire had spent the better part of the afternoon at the coffee shop, with Josh ordering another round of coffee for the two of them. Claire had not talked this much about literature in a long time. As she knew it bored many people to tears, she avoided inflicting this on her friends.

8

Singapore

Claire missed her running, or even simply walking about, in the three weeks she was on crutches. She had a regular route that started from a giant acacia tree just outside her condominium's gate, followed by stretches of *ixora*s, and then the grassy football field next to a housing development board, or 'HDB' as the locals would call it. Tall trees in particular reminded her to either slow down or run faster. They were the more stable visual elements of her run. Each session, though, was as distinct as the birds and tropical creatures along the way, like the mynahs that swooped down to fight for a biscuit crumb before her, or the snail that she had almost stepped on. Claire felt energized only after this outdoor routine. She never achieved this sense of satisfaction when running on a treadmill in an air-conditioned room, even though both her office and condominium buildings had gym facilities.

    Today, being the first time without her crutches, she could entertain the thought of running again. She excitedly went to her balcony and gazed at the starting point of her regular run. Just a few more days and she could be out there on her trail again. Before returning inside, she paused to inspect her plants arranged neatly on a rack on the side. They were mostly succulents and orchids in small pots, a few leafy crotons, and a couple of tall palm plants in the corner. They looked healthy, thanks to Anna, who had watered them regularly when she was here and to JM who had refilled the drip tubes buried in each pot, a hack that she learned from the Internet to keep her plants hydrated even when she was travelling.

She was about to pick up one of the succulents when Melanie called.

'Claire, I have some good news for you,' she greeted.

She would be coming to Asia in two weeks to be with Frank, her husband, who was scheduled to give a lecture series in Bangkok. They planned to drop by Singapore for three days after Frank's lecture.

'That's a pleasant surprise. I thought I wouldn't be seeing you any time soon as my trip to New York got cancelled,' Claire said.

'Frank's lecture was announced some time ago. But I hadn't planned on joining him at the time, because I wanted to be in New York for you,' Melanie replied.

Before she knew it, Claire met an excited Melanie in the lobby restaurant of a hotel along Orchard Road. Melanie hugged her tightly for what seemed like hours before finally straightening to introduce Claire to Frank.

'I was here ten years ago, but it was a different place then. I don't remember seeing so many skyscrapers and shiny malls back then,' Frank said, as he adjusted his steel-rimmed glasses.

'Indeed. There's something new every year. There's the Sail in Marina Bay and soon we'll have the Universal Studios in Sentosa among other attractions. Even I can't keep up with the latest,' Claire replied.

Claire soon found out that Frank was passionate about economic events and the much-speculated power shift to Asia. They talked about this throughout their two-hour dinner. Frank then excused himself to make a few calls in their room and let Melanie and Claire carry on with their coffee.

'I'm sorry I couldn't be here sooner. God knows I really wanted to be here when you had the accident,' Melanie said.

'No worries. Mama immediately came to the rescue. Besides, it was only a minor accident, although I had to walk around in crutches for three weeks,' Claire replied.

'I know, I know, but it would have been different if I were here myself.' She paused for a while before adding, 'Claire, there's something I wanted to tell you. I've already told Nate and Melissa about you. Ah, it was awkward, for me especially. But I thank the Lord for blessing me with understanding and non-judgmental children.'

'Frank seems nice, so I'm not surprised your children are equally nice,' Claire looked at her empty cup, trying to formulate her thoughts, but instead blurted out the foremost question in her mind, 'May I ask you a question? Apart from half-expecting me to knock on your door when I had turned eighteen, were you ever curious about me?' She had wanted to ask this all along, but could not find the right place or time. Even now, where they were, was neither the right time nor place. But Claire felt there would never be a perfect one anyway.

'You have no idea of what and how much I had been through. The first few years were the hardest. There wasn't a single day I didn't think of you. Showing up in class during the day, as if everything was fine, while being tortured at night, had almost taken its toll on me.' Melanie took a deep breath.

'This sounds weird coming from me,' Claire said, trying to detach herself from the discussion, 'but I wouldn't know how to cope in that situation myself.'

'I was probably depressed for a while, only I didn't go for any counselling or clinical diagnosis at that time. I didn't know any better. Things were different then. We didn't have much access to information. Anyway, I spent the better part of that semester in my dorm room, until my roommates began to get worried. So I started going out, though, at some point, going out for the sake of it felt aimless. Empty. Later on, I realized that, having given up so much, I needed to make the best of my situation,' Melanie said softly.

'What was the turning point?' Claire asked, now more curious than emotional. She enjoyed reading human-interest stories especially about overcoming great obstacles. It never occurred to her, though, that one day the story she would be listening to would be her birth mother's.

'I passed out in a student hall after an all-night drinking binge. I was rushed to the hospital where a doctor set me right. From then on, I tried to find solace by telling myself that you were in the hands of people who would take care of you far better than I ever could. I kept reminding myself that your parents are warm and kind-hearted, especially Dino,' she said, trying hard to suppress the tears that gathered in the corners of her eyes.

'But what convinced you that they'd truly take good care of me?' Claire asked.

'I did a lot of research, read tons of newspapers and microfilms about your clan. Unlike the other political dynasties then, your family rarely appeared in the news, and I mean it in a good way. Although there were profiles of your grandparents and great-grandfather and articles about your grandmother in Sunday magazines and in the lifestyle sections, there were no corruption charges or feuds with other political dynasties. I gave you up then, Claire, but I did it for your own good as much as all the reasons that your grandmother made me believe in. Besides, you are their own blood, so I've always believed that they would give you only the best,' Melanie paused, waiting for her tears to stop.

Claire felt sad for Melanie but, inexplicably, sadder for herself. It occurred to her that, had it not been for her grandmother's skilful manipulation at the time, Claire's questionable birth could have generated a lot of talk and shone an unwanted spotlight on their clan.

'When I went home after my graduation, everyone in my village was proud of me. It was the one moment my father had been waiting for. I've never seen my parents so proud. But deep down, it was an empty victory for me. I did not feel any sense of triumph. It was a sad time, perhaps second only to the time I handed you to Dino and

Anna, after knowing how it felt to have you in my arms and hold you close to my heart.'

Claire had more questions, but she could see that Melanie looked exhausted.

Claire was restless that night, waking up every now and then. She did not want to watch any more TV programmes or read any more books because she needed to sleep properly in preparation for an early meeting at the office the next day. She walked over to the bay window in her room, parted the curtains, and sat in a corner, clutching her knees to her chin. Her condominium unit was on the twelfth floor of a ten-year-old building and from here she could see the distant harbour. On a bright day, she could see the ships waiting to be berthed or getting ready to sail. Tonight, she could see the distant lights from the berthed ships. While appearing calm and collected during dinner with Melanie, Claire allowed repressed emotions to surface in the solitude of her room. Currently, she felt like an overburdened cargo ship.

Melanie was but a victim of her circumstances. She had tried to make the best out of the cards she was dealt with. At times, though, Claire wondered what might have been if Melanie had not given her up and had raised her herself, what it would have been like to have had someone she could talk to openly regardless of the subject matter. Her grandmother had certainly been attentive, but Claire had always felt too deferent to express a different opinion. As for Anna, she had always been present for Claire and regularly introduced her to activities like baking, sewing and even nail-painting. But Claire had always felt something was missing even before she discovered that Anna was not her biological mother. This became more apparent when Claire saw how close her friends were with their mothers. Pia and her mother, for instance, bonded over shopping. They would gush over shoes and seemingly over every other thing whenever they were in the mall together. She also saw how Trisha, another friend at university, enjoyed crafting with her mum and would happily swop books and magazines with her. Claire realized that, while Anna may not have been as engaging as the other mums, Anna was truly a good person with the best of intentions. Anna never talked negatively about another person, even about her household helpers, which was perhaps why her helpers were loyal to her. Claire resolved to start thinking of Anna in a better light especially after the warm moments she had shared with her during her last visit.

On the other hand, if Melanie had not given her up, Claire would not have the financial security of being a Rosales. Claire never heard of any squabble over money in their house or in her grandmother's. Her family was not as wealthy as those dynastic families she kept hearing about in the news, but Claire was not ignorant of her privileges. She had realized this early on while at university, where many of her classmates had not even travelled out of the main island, let alone outside of the country. There were days, too, when a frappuccino was a big decision for her classmates—some could not afford one, but would still politely decline her offer to buy it for them.

At times, it occurred to Claire that she might have been too harsh on Melanie. Should not Ric be held more accountable? After all, he was the one who had taken advantage of Melanie's youth and naïvete. But then, Claire did not want to waste any headspace on Ric. If she had her way, Claire would not want to see Ric again, talk to him again, or even devote an iota of her mind on him. She wished he were someone she did not have to deal with, someone inconsequential who had no bearing on any facet of her life. She could not even begin to consider any paternal relationship with him. She could not accept a liar for a father. She could not accept being the daughter of an adulterer, a serial womanizer, especially one who pretended to be wholesome in public. Ric was a hypocrite of the highest order.

#

Claire and Melanie met again that Saturday, this time at Dempsey Hill. 'Thank God it is not too humid today. I don't think you'd have been able to walk so far otherwise,' Claire told Melanie as they sat for lunch.

'I know. I love walking and I enjoy it better in good weather. Today is perfect. Unfortunately Frank could not join us because he's meeting a friend from his university days,' Melanie said. 'I didn't know the other blocks around here also house the art galleries. Left on my own, I would have gone only to the home décor shops and the gallery where we saw that Basquiat.'

'That Basquiat. For 380,000 . . . euros. Isn't it insane? It looks like a mere collage to me,' Claire was incredulous.

'You'd be surprised at how much his most famous painting sold for at an auction. Twenty-six million dollars,' Melanie raised an eyebrow.

'Seriously,' Claire's jaw dropped. 'I'd never be able to afford one even if I worked night and day for the rest of my life. In two or more lifetimes.'

'Come on, you're still young. You can start saving now,' Melanie teased.

'Or I could start buying lottery tickets,' Claire smiled. She was amused at Melanie who got excited whenever they talked about visual arts. Melanie knew the works not only of classical artists but also of modern and contemporary ones, including those from Southeast Asia—from Elmer Borlongan of the Philippines to the young Eko Nugroho from Indonesia.

'I'm glad you chose this area for lunch. I love galleries and museums. I know it doesn't sound cool. Nate or Melissa would never be seen with me in museums even if I paid them to do so,' Melanie shared.

'Weirdly, I enjoy going to museums. In fact, whenever I travel on my own, I always visit a museum or two.' Claire was probably the only person she knew who had a bucket list of museums.

'What's your favourite one?' Melanie leaned forward to listen.

'The big ones in New York, London, and Paris, are quite impressive but, for some reason, I've enjoyed visiting smaller museums more. I particularly like the Peggy Guggenheim Collection in Venice and the Museo Thyssen-Bornemisza in Madrid, perhaps because I had more time to linger and savour their exhibits. Most importantly I didn't get lost in those two museums,' she replied.

'That's not unusual. I, obviously, love the The Metropolitan Museum of Art or The Met and of course the Museum of Modern Art or MoMA, though I think I like the Rijks more. I can stare at the Rembrandts and Vermeers all day long. And of course it helps that the Van Gogh Museum is just a short walk away,' Melanie shared. 'I can talk for hours about my favourite Dutch artists, but I don't want to bore you, my dear,' she added.

Earlier, Claire attributed her love of the arts to Gloria's influence, but now she realized that it might have come genetically from Melanie's side too. Both Gloria and Melanie were equally knowledgeable about the arts, though each in their own distinct way. Her grandmother had been keen on the aesthetics and the painting style, while Melanie knew the stories and inspiration behind many masterpieces.

'I didn't realize we've been talking for almost two hours now. I need to make a quick call. It won't take five minutes,' Claire said stopping her phone alarm, which reminded her of her scheduled call, before stepping out into the empty courtyard.

Upon her return to their table, Claire noticed the change in Melanie's expression. Melanie no longer looked the excited art connoisseur that she was just moments ago. 'We're going to Cebu for a couple of days to check on my parents,' she said.

'Wow, you must be excited,' Claire beamed at her.

'Yes and no,' Melanie replied softly.

'I would be if I were you. I love Cebu. I love the food. They make the best lechon. But what don't you like about going?' she asked.

'Claire, my parents still don't know about you,' Melanie said with a pained expression.

Claire almost gasped but managed to check her kneejerk reaction. She looked out of the window as she tried to compose her thoughts. Suddenly she felt as though she was some contraband that needed to be hidden. She mentally cursed the entire world. And because she could not verbalize what she felt, she took a sip of water and waited for Melanie to continue.

'I never had a chance to tell them about you in the past. If it were up to just me, I'd take you along now so that you could meet them,' Melanie added. 'There is no way I can make amends for the sins of the past. But you must know that I have always been thinking of you, especially on your birthdays. Some say that time can erode memories. The brain might forget but the heart does not. You were with me in my most important moments. On my wedding day. When I gave birth to Nate and later to Melissa. During my career promotions. After all it was because of you that I had to strive hard,' Melanie started tearing up again.

Claire, herself, was trying to quell the lump that was growing in her throat. 'I thought my biggest trial in life was when I had to cancel my wedding. But whatever pain I had felt then, paled to Lola's death. And before I could even get over the more recent loss, here comes the biggest question—of my identity,' Claire's voice started to shake, but she kept herself from crying.

'God. I'm so sorry. I never wished so much pain on anyone, let alone on my own daughter,' Melanie hugged Claire tightly. After a while Melanie straightened up. She wiped away all traces of tears, took a deep breath, and drank the remaining water from her glass.

Claire looked around and was relieved to see that the restaurant was not crowded this time of day. She wanted to say a few more things but did not want to risk seeing Melanie cry again, especially in public.

'Please don't ever feel that you are alone in this. Now that we've found each other again, neither of us should go on this journey alone,' Melanie said, placing one hand on her chest.

Claire nodded, impressed at Melanie's ability to express her emotions freely. While Melanie could be spontaneous, she was also thoughtful and purposeful in her actions. She always checked before she did anything that might affect Claire. On the other hand, if Melanie were less involved, it would have been easier for Claire to go on with her life and pretend that she did not know about Melanie's existence. Not many people knew about Claire's struggle and she dreaded telling others about this. She did not even have the courage to break it to JM and Mike by herself. All her guilt flooded back as she recalled how concerned JM had been about her during his last visit and how she had been withholding the whole truth from him all that time. She also had to tell her friends. They would not stop being her friends just because of this discovery, but she nonetheless worried about being judged because of this.

'I have an idea. Why don't you come and visit us this Thanksgiving?' Melanie offered.

'As in this year?' Claire asked, snapping out of her introspection.

'Yes, this year. Both Nate and Melissa will also be home then and it would be a great time for you to meet each other. I'm sure you will find many things in common. Not the museums for sure. But Nate is a bookworm and Melissa is into running too. And they're both eagerly looking forward to see you.'

'I'd love to meet them too, but let me check my travel schedule first. I might be in Amsterdam around that time. Wait, maybe I could fly out from there that weekend. Let's see,' she said.

'Please do your best. I really want you to finally meet your siblings,' Melanie begged. 'I'll take care of your plane tickets.'

'It's not a question of that. It's more a question of time. If I'm able to take time off from work, I'll definitely find my way to New York on Thanksgiving,' Claire tried to be more enthusiastic as she said this. But part of her also hesitated to commit. Claire would always be an outsider however much Melanie tried to bring her into the fold. Melanie had an orderly life with her tightly-knit family. Claire was not part of their shared memories, their internal jokes, or even the lingua franca that only they could understand. She could easily imagine them to be the most rational bunch of people, the types who did not tolerate any dramas in the house. Conversely, she could not imagine Nate and Melissa in the colourful world in which she grew up, they did not fit in the everyday crowd at her grandmother's place, the fanfares during elections and festivals, and the public life that her older relatives were used to. 'I'll let you know early next week,' she said.

Claire called a cab and dropped Melanie off at her hotel. From there she decided to go to Books Kinokuniya via Scotts Road. She was in deep thought and absent-mindedly gave a two-dollar bill to an elderly lady selling pocket-sized tissues without taking the packets that she had bought. She felt disoriented among the weekend crowd in the underpass. She avoided being in crowded places as much as she could but had forgotten that this part of Orchard Road could be the most congested place in Singapore. Coming from the Rosales clan, to whom a large audience, especially during elections, meant a good thing, she should have gotten used to it by now. Then it occurred to her that she was spared from public life owing largely to Dino and Anna. She had always assumed that her parents naturally preferred to be low-key, but it occurred to her now that it was probably because of her that they had maintained low profiles amid the swirl of politics. It could be one more of their many sacrifices for her. But why would they choose such an uneventful life? This bit remained a puzzle to her. Claire had always assumed that she knew everything about her family. She took everyone and every word at face value. But now she started questioning what motivated each member of her family. Why did they behave the way they did. Was it money on Anna's part? What about Dino? Was it to regain his place in the clan and to ensure he got his fair share of the Rosales fortune? How could Claire even think of such thoughts about her well-meaning parents? Once more, Claire mentally berated herself for these wayward thoughts.

9

Singapore

The days before Claire's Amsterdam trip were doubly hectic compared to her regular days in the office. One of her key clients urgently needed a more detailed annual analysis of his company's brands, likely triggered by a declining trend that Claire had pointed out in the last quarterly report. This unexpected work-stream led to even later hours at work. Claire's only consolation was seeing the office atmosphere seemingly back to its less sombre mood. Marc and Rinka were upbeat as usual. Marie, their administrative assistant, would break into her Broadway songs now and then, humming cheerful tunes these days, a welcome change from her *Les Miserables* repertoire the week before.

As her usual morning routine, Claire went into the pantry to refill her water bottle. She bumped into Chris, who was on his way out. 'How was your weekend?' he asked, steadying the coffee mug he was holding.

'It was great. I finally got to watch *A Little Night Music*,' she said.

'Oh yeah? I've heard about that but haven't had a chance to watch. Sondheim, right?'

'Yep, I totally loved this one. How was your weekend?'

'Had a relaxing one by the pool. The first time in weeks,' he replied, glancing at his watch. 'I need to get into a funnel review now, but let's catch up later in the day.' He still looked uptight, though less haggard than he did the previous week.

Claire could not wait for Chris to fully revert to his normal self. She missed their earlier camaraderie, one that grew out of the long working hours they had spent together over the years in various efforts to win customers. She missed the group celebrations, particularly after the challenging wins against strong competition. Last year was a banner year for the company as they had unexpectedly won more accounts that led to more celebrations. In contrast, this year was bleak. Their management and operations team did not seem prepared to handle and maintain several high-profile accounts simultaneously. They had not anticipated the difficulty that came with the so-called 'prestige' of having more blue-chip accounts in the company credentials. Some of the newer clients had started complaining because of delivery gaps. Earlier, when the complaints were milder, Chris thought they came with the territory. He would gripe every now and then about the ridiculous demands, but would nonetheless address them, eventually appeasing the clients. Recently though Chris had a heated argument that led to a key client threatening to pull his account out. It grew into a graver issue that needed Chris's global chief executive officer to intervene.

At lunch, Claire met Marc and Rinka at their favourite bistro in their office building. Marc chose a spot farthest from the entrance. As soon as their food arrived, Marc started the talk about Chris. 'Well, at least now he leaves his office door open sometimes. Earlier it was completely shut the entire day. Some of my reports were delayed because I couldn't talk to him for weeks,' Marc said as he drizzled the dressing on his Mediterranean salad.

'Even I was scared of his scowls,' Rinka chimed in, 'and I kept dreading that he'd ask me to redo things for the nth time.'

'It must have been most difficult for you as you've been working with him more closely than any of us,' Claire noted.

'You could say that. But today his mood seems better, perhaps because Bateman & Cooper has calmed down finally,' Rinka said.

'How did he manage to tame that beast of a client?' Marc asked.

'The gods in the UK had to promise them freebies as part of service recovery. Those freebies are the reason I've been extremely busy lately,' Rinka said.

'Is that why you haven't been traveling in the past month or so?' Claire asked.

'Yep, I had to cancel my trip to Osaka to complete the dashboard that B&C wanted,' Rinka added.

'At least that saga is coming to an end now. Speaking of travels, when and where is your next trip?' Marc asked Claire.

'This Monday. For Project Tulip. Will you be in any of the project meetings?' Claire asked.

'It's not confirmed yet. But I'm on standby. I might go a few days before the pitch presentation itself.'

'I hope you'll be able to join. We haven't gone on the same trip in a long time. Amsterdam would be more fun with you around,' she said.

'Wait, wait, how do I officially become part of the Tulip team?' Rinka pouted.

'You don't have to join on an official basis, Rinka. Aren't you due for your annual leave anyway?' Marc asked.

'Good idea, Marc. Yes, Rinka, why don't you do that? Come even if it's just for a weekend. I'm sure you have enough airline miles for redemption,' Claire cheered up at the thought.

'Cool, I'm excited all of a sudden. Claire, I can room in with you if ever, right?' Rinka brimmed with excitement. While she looked conservative with her characteristic long dresses, Rinka was the most outgoing and adventurous Japanese that Claire had ever met. After her university days in London, Rinka had travelled practically everywhere and had done some solo trips, like Macchu Pichu, too.

'Of course, Rinka,' Claire replied. 'It goes without saying.'

'What about me?' Marc asked.

'You? You'll need to find someone else to bunk with or else Chris will give me that suspicious look,' Claire teased back.

'I would not blab about it. Come on, I'm not a kiss-and-tell guy,' Marc winked.

'Marc, you better read the office policy again, okay? The last time I checked, there is a long paragraph clearly indicating that colleagues of the opposite gender canNOT and must NOT share a room.'

Marc pretended to be ignorant of this and was acting disappointed. 'Bummer. Why can't you ignore the rules just for a couple of nights? If the situation were reversed, I'd happily do it for you,' Marc said, before downing the last drop of his Coke Zero in can.

Claire rolled her eyes knowing Marc was merely teasing. She knew about Marc's gender orientation. Marc had revealed this during one of their coffee sessions.

'So, when? What dates are you looking at,' Rinka was already scrolling through her iPhone.

'You can go any time in the next three weeks, except during the last weekend of November—I might go to New York then,' Claire suddenly remembered.

'Why don't we do first week of December then?' Rinka wanted to finalize the dates.

'Works for me. First week of December it is,' Marc replied. 'Now I need to go charm the bosses so Marie can finalize my itinerary.'

10

Amsterdam

The flight to Amsterdam was bumpy and Claire could not sleep even when she had transformed her seat into a flat bed. She watched *The Royal Tenenbaums*, a movie that reaffirmed her admiration of Wes Anderson. She marvelled at how this quirky family that had been in shambles ultimately found redemption. She watched *Lost in Translation* and it instantly became her favourite movie of all time. She could relate to the theme of dislocation and ennui. She had been living away from home for many years now but had never really reflected on how she felt about it. Her transfer to Singapore came when she needed it most and at that time she chose to be preoccupied with her relocation than entertain other emotions. But now with the movie as stimulus, she could not help but think of all the things she was missing, and missing out on, by being away from home. How many birthday celebrations? Weddings? Baptisms? How many mini-reunions or family trips? How many times had she wished to be with her family when one of the members fell ill?

Thoughts of time being linear came back to Claire. She wished that one's birth certificate came with an outline of one's lifeline, and pre-marked with peaks and troughs all the way to the end. If she had that kind of a map, she would know how long she had yet to be in this suspended stage. She was definitely out of the trough now as far as grieving over her grandmother was concerned, though at times anger took its place. On the other hand, she was below the peak yet with this latest burden about her true parentage. She once knew how it felt to be carefree, joyful and elated. She once knew these feelings in their purest form, when they were as yet untainted by all the knowledge that she had now. With all the progress that man had made in scientific prediction and modelling, why had no one invented a tool that could predict one's immediate future more precisely? If she had had a map and a predicting tool, she would know how her present quandary would be resolved. But how did she want things to be resolved? Was a mere recognition from Ric going to be enough? Did she simply want the rest of the clan to acknowledge the truth about her and resume business as usual after that? Before her thoughts became any more esoteric, Claire decided to switch off the entertainment screen and tried to read another travel magazine. Then she decided to switch the screen back on and watched *Eternal Sunshine of the Spotless Mind*, hoping it would cheer her up—but some of the scenes saddened her and being in full-on empathetic mode it almost made her cry. There was only one other time when she had cried over a movie and this was many years ago while watching *Beaches* at one of her sleepovers with Pia.

Claire arrived in Amsterdam on a Sunday and checked in at the Marriott, which was centrally located and not too far from Vondelpark, something that had excited her initially because she could do her daily run in the park, although now she realized she could not do much in the gloomy weather that greeted her. Besides, she might not find the time as she had yet to complete her section of the pitch proposal for a global skincare brand headquartered in the Netherlands. In her first week, the only time she had managed to step away from her workstation was when her Dutch colleagues took her out for dinner near the Jordaan district, a short distance from their office. And dinner was practically all they could do anyway as Claire had a low tolerance threshold for cold temperature despite the several layers of thermal wears that she had on. Her Dutch counterparts pushed more drinks her way to 'help her adjust to the weather' but, as a rule, Claire never drank more than two pegs of alcohol when on a work trip.

Chris also arrived in Amsterdam the following week and Claire fell into a pattern of having breakfast with him. This morning, Chris seemed almost back to normal, as he was now capable of laughing, especially when he recalled some Dilbert comic strips that he shared with Claire. His jolly mood was sustained during the cab ride to the office and Claire also started relaxing when she realized this. On Chris's last night in Amsterdam, the Dutch team took them out to dinner once again, which they eventually capped off at the hotel bar. When it was only the two of them left at the bar, Chris started alluding to his personal issues.

'So it wasn't because of B&C,' Claire couldn't help but ask what everyone else back in Singapore thought was the reason for Chris's issues.

'I was worried about that, too, but to a much lesser extent. I've dealt with bigger client issues before,' he said. It turned out he had marital problems. Despite their good work rapport Claire did not want to ask him about his personal situation though their conversation eventually veered into this. 'Sara was not the same person I met at university,' he added referring to his wife.

'Don't we all change at some point?' Claire said.

'Absolutely. But we all want to change for the better, don't we? Hers wasn't in the best direction I suppose. In fact, if it were not for Mandy, we might not have lasted that long anyway,' Chris replied.

'What happened exactly?' she could not resist but ask after all.

'Sara claimed I'd lost interest in her. That I'd turned into a workaholic, drained of any energy when it came to family life and any energy I had left was spent solely on Mandy,' he sighed in between sips of his single-malt whisky. 'Then of course, Sara started meeting all these ladies-who-lunch types, the expat wives. She could not help but be competitive. She had become frivolous trying to keep up with them. In the end we didn't seem to be looking in the same direction.'

'What do you mean?' Claire probed hesitantly. A part of her did not want to hear any more because sometimes knowing so much about a person could become a burden. Besides, she did not know what to do with all the information. At the same time she wanted to show Chris her support.

'Last summer, for instance, we had to go on separate holidays. I went to a Habitat for Humanities project in Cambodia because I had committed to it much earlier, while she went to Maldives with her friends. Mandy was torn between us, but in the end she decided to go with Sara because some of Mandy's friends were there too,' he paused to finish his drink.

Chris doted on his seven-year-old daughter, Mandy, so it pained him to be separated from her, as she was now in Sara's custody. 'Ah, I should not be bothering you with these things. I mean you seem so put together, no drama in there, right, Claire?' Chris said.

'That's what you think,' Claire laughed a bit louder than normal. She wanted to empathize with Chris, but did not know how. She felt out of her depth when talking about serious relationships when they unravelled like this. From out of the blue she started recounting her own break up. As she did so, she felt detached from the situation as though the whole affair did not happen to her. She did not feel any pain at the recollection. At some point she even laughed at the silliness of it all and for allowing herself to be tormented by it back then.

'That guy is a bloody asshole. Thank goodness you found out about his dodgy side sooner. Imagine being stuck in a marriage that you would have ultimately detested,' Chris put his glass down almost with a thud as he said this.

'That was many summers ago. I'm well over it now. More than anything, I mourned the wasted time in the aftermath. Back then, I thought it was the end of the world for me. With distance and time, though, I soon realized that it was only a blip in my lifeline,' she replied.

'Absolutely. But, wait . . . if you haven't gone out with anyone since then, there seems to be a problem still, no?' he probed.

'No, I don't think so. It's more the lack of time. I have way too many projects, and you should feel guilty for that,' she tried to ease the tension.

'Am I being a slave-driver now?' Chris frowned.

'No, of course not. The truth is, Chris, I have not had a chance to meet Prince Charming yet. I go on dates, but I haven't met the right guy yet. Not that I'm in any rush,' she finished the last of her drink and shook her head when Chris asked if she wanted another glass.

'Hmmm. Perhaps you're being too picky? I can name a couple of eligible and decent guys in our department alone,' he said.

'Are you sure you could handle the complication of office romance between your team members on top of your financial targets?' Claire teased.

'Come to think of it, an office romance might brighten up the office. That could be interesting. Though perhaps not if you are the one involved,' he replied.

Claire frowned and drew a question mark.

'In the first place I don't see you getting into messy affairs. On second thoughts, those guys in the office might not be eligible enough for you.'

'You seem to be talking in riddles.'

'To put it simply, Miss Rosales, I think you deserve better than any of those guys on the seventeenth floor. Now, shall we call it a night? Unfortunately, I have a flight to catch first thing in the morning,' he replied, before signalling the waiter for the cheque.

Claire was glad that their old camaraderie seemed to be back. While she had always respected boundaries between work and personal affairs, she did not mind some bonding time, especially as she and Chris had been working together for more than three years now. These small interactions helped to make her feel more connected. After all, she was not a robot that was expected to nod and produce reports promptly, without questions or complaints, whenever someone pressed the 'work' button.

11

Amsterdam

The brain is an organ unto itself. Someone once likened it to a non-stop radio station. However hard she tried, Claire could not empty her mind of all the thoughts that kept streaming in. She had yet to understand why memories that had been dormant for many years came flooding back now. She got up with a headache that she tried to ignore as she went about her morning routine. She checked her phone and saw several messages from her family and close friends as usual. There was one from Chris checking how she was. Not that she drank much the night before, but the fact that he remembered to check on her made her feel important. After replying to urgent messages, she tried to make coffee but she felt dizzy. She grabbed the bottled water on the nightstand and drank as much as she could before leaning back against the headboard. She steadied herself and tried to repress any rising panic at the thought that she might pass out again like earlier at the Botanic Gardens. Syncope. She detested that word. She focused on her breathing and her breathing alone. The nausea eventually passed but she didn't want to take a risk by rushing to the office, so she decided to work from the hotel. She called room service for her breakfast and when it was delivered she tried to sip her coffee more slowly instead of gulping it down as she had been doing in the past few days. She also lingered over her toast and omelette, though this time, it was because of lack of appetite. Perhaps this episode of dizziness was due to the continuous long hours at work in the past two weeks and the extra peg of vodka last night. Perhaps her micronutrient levels were down again. She must remember to take her vitamin and dietary supplements after breakfast. But aside from the dizziness she also felt unusually low this morning. In all the years since it happened, she had scarcely talked to anyone about her cancelled wedding. The chat with Chris was rather unusual for her. While she did not feel the pain anymore, recounting the whole episode again had somehow stirred her subconscious. Away from home on a gloomy winter day, memories of when she was twenty-five and on the brink of getting married flooded back.

#

Santa Rosa, Valle Viejo

The year was 2005, and no one was more excited about Claire's engagement than Gloria who had wanted to be on every detail of the wedding preparation. Gloria had immediately gotten in touch with the archbishop of Valle Viejo for him to officiate the wedding. Mimi, who was miles away, was not to be outdone. She had volunteered to be the principal wedding coordinator. As though she was born for this role, she had come fully equipped with all the latest tools, including a customized journal for all the appointments, tons of bridal magazines, magnetic mood boards, and other paraphernalia. Anna had happily focused on the floral decorations and most importantly on the design of the gown that she, as mother of the bride, would be wearing. As Anna would be walking beside the bride, all eyes would naturally be on her too, she had explained. It had been three months of happy chaos for the women in Claire's family.

But things had taken a surprising turn when Claire decided she could not go through with the wedding after all. Over breakfast at the Rosales House after Christmas, Claire had mustered her courage and told her family, 'The wedding is off.'

Everyone had gasped as though on cue. Claire could still remember each face in freeze-frame. It was not too different from a scene in a Bollywood soap opera when the camera would zoom in on a character's face right after someone had dropped a bombshell. Multiply that expression ten times.

'But what happened, hija?' Gloria had asked with finesse, concern written all over her face.

'Lola, it's embarrassing,' Claire had said. She had planned to be brief and not to disclose unnecessary details though she should have known that where her family was concerned, one could not evade a discussion that easily.

'What did he do to you? I'm going to give that guy what he deserves, and probably more,' Mike had immediately gotten up and gone over to her side.

'Please, everyone. Calm down. Let's hear what Claire has to say first.' It seemed Mimi was the only one with a cool head at that time.

Claire could not lift her head.

Dino, usually quiet, had gotten up as well and told Claire that she should not feel pressured to explain and that they would understand if she chose to not disclose the details. What was important, he had added, was that Claire made the right decision. They, the Rosales clan, respected this.

'Was there a third party?' asked JM in a more controlled voice than Mike's.

'Worse than that,' Claire had finally lifted her head. 'I found a Zeus club card in his wallet. I thought only dirty old men would go to such seedy night clubs with those huge posters of scantily clad entertainers. He's been a member of that sleazy place for some time now,' Claire had replied sadly.

'Oh my God. That club along Timog Avenue with the blown-up photos of women prancing around in G-strings? Goodness. I've heard from my friends that all those vertical dancers eventually end up in horizontal positions. I'm sorry for the lack of better words, but those dancers are just glorified sex workers. They're a disgrace to womenfolk. And those dirty patrons are despicable, taking advantage of those women,' Mimi had shaken her head in complete disgust.

'Precisely. I can't, for the life of me, fathom why a guy like Jason went there, not just once, but many times and even became a member,' Claire had cringed at that thought.

'He's sick. What a jerk. He'll definitely get it from me, too,' JM had said with a clenched jaw.

'No, don't waste your time on him. He begged for forgiveness, but his fooling around even just before our wedding was simply unacceptable. Imagine what he could do after the wedding. He said the card wasn't his and he was only keeping it on behalf of his friend, Edward. Eww! I don't want to be near him ever again,' Claire had finally vented.

'At least you found it sooner rather than later,' Mimi had replied. *'He clearly doesn't deserve you.'*

Ric had merely nodded after everyone had affirmed Claire's decision to cancel the wedding. *'Are you sure you don't want him tracked down?'* he had asked, before getting up.

'Yes, I'm very sure of that, Uncle Ric. I don't want anyone in the family to be near him. He's beyond detestable,' Claire had added.

'I knew it. I couldn't place my finger on it earlier, but somehow I had sensed that something was off with him. He might have been the smartest guy in your MBA batch, but clearly he has moral issues,' JM had said.

It had taken a while for everyone to be convinced to leave Jason alone. *'He's not worth any effort or thought from this family. He is a scum of the lowest order. I don't want anyone of us to be contaminated by his dirt,'* Claire had hoped to end the discussion already.

On the drive to Buena Vista the next day, Dino had tried his best to make light of the situation. *'I'm sure your mama is disappointed not so much with the wedding cancellation but with the fact that she won't be able to wear that gown after all,'* he said.

'I know, Dad. Mama was so excited about her gown,' Claire had said. *'But I think Mama should be able to recover soon. I'm more worried about Lola.'*

'Your Lola is definitely hurt, but more for your sake than for herself. She is a veteran of life's struggles. She'll weather this like the many storms that came before.'

'That's precisely why I found it hard to break the news to her. Lola had been through so much already.'

'Mama was certainly saddened by the news. Who wouldn't be? But Claire, we don't want you to end up with such a scoundrel.'

'It's such a big waste of money though, Daddy.'

'Let that dirty, rotten man clean up the mess he has created,' Dino had said.

'What about the hotels and transport that Lola has already paid for?'

'I had a chat with Mama before we left yesterday, and that's the last thing on her mind. In fact she's thinking of going back to Manila with you after the New Year celebrations.'

'I wish I'd found out about this mess sooner. I could have saved everyone the trouble.'

'Look, hija, if everything was within our control and we were not allowed to make any mistakes, we'd be no different from robots.'

'But Daddy, this is a horrible mistake. An epic fail. I've caused our family a lot of hassle and embarrassment.' It was one of those times when Claire had wished she could hide under a blanket forever.

Dino had parked the car and she turned to rest her head on his shoulder. When her tears had stopped, Dino had gone around to open her door. 'Claire, I think the worst is over. You've already told the clan about it and that was the most important step. Now we're all here to help you get over this episode,' Dino had reminded her.

'I know, Daddy. Right now though, I wish I could be swallowed by a sink hole.'

'We are here for you and we are the ones that matter to you. If anyone must fall and crumble, it should be your ex-fiancé.' Claire had known then that Dino was furious. The fact that he could not even mention the name of her ex-fiancé was more than enough indication.

'I'll do my best, Daddy.'

'Remember that you are a Rosales. Don't let anyone hurt you or make you feel any less of yourself,' he had finally said.

After her family's assurance of their support, Claire had felt bold enough to face the likely barrage in her office the following week. Gloria, Anna and Mimi had gone with her to Manila. Anna had ensured that

Claire's choice of comfort food was available throughout the week. Gloria and Mimi had attended to the logistics issues, cancelling all the wedding-related reservations and rentals they had made earlier. Gloria had stayed on for another month until everything was settled to her satisfaction. Dino and Anna had also visited her on weekends. In the end, the women in her family had managed the crisis without Claire having lifted a finger. Before this chapter in her life, Claire had not seen her family come together for her in full force like this. With this incident, she had realized what loyalty meant to the Rosales clan. Her family was her fortress and she knew she would not be crushed easily for as long as they were around. If her family had ever done anything unjust to her in the past, she would have absolved them right there and then.

A few months after the wedding cancellation, Claire had received an offer to transfer to Singapore. Her family had welcomed the news and had encouraged her to accept the offer. *'I'm so proud of you*, hija. *You're a Rosales, no doubt,'* Gloria had beamed with pride as they sat together for coffee one weekend afternoon at their Makati apartment.

'Wow, this is wonderful news. Congrats. A new place can help you get over unpleasant experiences faster,' JM had said as he opened a box of Portuguese egg tarts, a favourite of Gloria and now Claire's too.

'I'm well over that incident. Don't worry. I was more concerned about the mess in the aftermath, but Lola and Auntie Mimi cleaned it all up ever so efficiently.'

'We learn from experience as Lola loves to say. Now you have a rule number one: Check the guy's wallet on your first date,' JM had chuckled at his own wisecrack. Claire could not help but laugh too, seeing that even her grandmother had understood the joke.

Over the next two months Claire had wrapped up her projects in the Philippines and prepared for her relocation to Singapore. She had flown in with Gloria and Anna to check on the apartments that her company had shortlisted. After viewing five properties, all three ladies had unanimously decided on a condominium unit in the upper East Coast area, this being near a park, a grocery and a few dining places. Gloria and Anna had insisted that Claire chose an apartment that had accessible dining areas knowing that Claire hardly cooked.

In the subsequent blur of activities, Claire had almost forgotten about her aborted wedding. Jason had attempted to reconnect several times, even enlisting his parents to talk on his behalf, but Claire had closed that chapter in her life firmly.

#

Sitting in her Amsterdam hotel room now, Claire realized that she was now more than five years away from that cancelled wedding. Yet, she found herself crying at that memory. The tears, though, were not because of any regrets from breaking up with Jason, for she had none. All the emotions related to Jason were reduced to ashes along with the gifts and mementos from him that she had shredded and burned that night when she had found out about the club card. Her sadness now was due more to the loss of a simpler world. She was crying more for her younger self. How at some point she had believed that she, too, would have a fairy-tale wedding and a happy family life thereafter. Through no fault of hers, that dream had collapsed. In that bygone world, too, she did not think twice about having to call either her grandmother or Dino to help her with even the simplest of issues. Back then there was no hesitation about leaning on her family for support. But knowing what she knew now, Claire was more conscious of making any demands on Dino and Anna. They were, after all, not her biological parents. They did not owe her anything and she did not have the birthright to demand anything from them.

12

Amsterdam

After that gloomy morning in her hotel room, Claire felt as though all her sorrows had flowed out with the tears—a long-overdue catharsis. In the afternoon, she went to the office feeling less encumbered. She was convinced now more than ever about the healing power of time. What a different perspective it had brought. How, in five years, so many things had changed but here she was, still standing. A survivor. She automatically lifted her chin when this thought occurred to her. Whatever came her way now would not be as important in another five years. She just needed to be strong enough to weather the current storm. It was just a matter of perspective, she whispered to herself. Somehow this change of mindset helped to prepare her for what the day held for her.

Now if only her work situation were always predictable, Claire could have lingered in her warrior state of mind. As it happened, her inner resolve was starting to erode from the real-time issues in the office. In the middle of reviewing the primary data on habits and practices that she needed for her analysis and report, Claire spotted inconsistencies and gross errors. The new data-set drastically contradicted trends that had been established earlier. She was furious at the research agency for not spotting this error earlier in the process, but her anger now could not undo the damage.

She still had to rework her report. She took a deep breath, picked up her laptop, and went into an empty huddle room and started calling her research agency partners and data support team. After more than two hours of conference calls, the teams involved finally aligned and agreed to rerun the data immediately.

After her conference calls, it dawned on Claire that this setback also meant she would not be able to go to New York for Thanksgiving. Her heart sank once more. She called Melanie to explain.

'Claire, that's a shame. We were all looking forward to your visit. Now I hate to see everyone's reaction when they hear this,' Melanie sounded downhearted.

'I'm really sorry. It's impossible to get away even just for a couple of days with the amount of work I must redo,' she explained.

'It's not your fault. But what can I say? I'm totally disappointed right now,' she said.

'I'm sorry, Melanie,' she sighed. 'I've spent so many nights working on that report. And I was hoping to finally meet Nate and Melissa.'

'It's really unfortunate, but don't worry about us now. I'm sure we'll find another chance to get together,' Melanie said. 'Wait, what about Christmas? Or New Year's Eve? You can actually be here for the countdown,' Melanie seemed to have regained her cheerfulness.

'I'd really love to do that,' Claire also cheered up at the idea of a countdown at Times Square, but she was also expected at Valle Viejo for the holidays. 'But first I need to check what the plans are at home,' she said with less enthusiasm. While she got excited about the Times Square countdown, a big part of her also wanted to be with Mimi, whom she had not seen for months now. Most importantly, she had always spent New Year's with Dino and Anna and the rest of the Rosales clan. She did not have the heart to break this tradition.

After days of long hours reworking her analysis, Claire heaved a big sigh of relief upon emailing the final report for Project Tulip. With the report out of the door now, Claire went down for breakfast at the office bulding's café. She chose a table that looked out into the street. It was yet another bleak day and she was starting to regret not having gone to New York. She was wondering if perhaps Nate and Melissa could potentially be her friends and confidantes—she needed someone she could talk to about her situation and perhaps either, or both, of the siblings could have been that someone. At times like now, she felt the disadvantages of being an only child and not having a sibling to talk to. Apart from Mimi and Dino, none of Claire's close relatives knew about her meetings with Melanie. She felt awkward about sharing this information even with Anna, though she knew she would have to share eventually. She also did not want JM and Mike to be drawn into this tangled web, but at the same time she could not keep things from her cousins much longer. She had started to feel hollow in her stomach whenever she was with them, knowing she was hiding a secret from them. There was, too, the bigger problem called Ric, but Claire had decided earlier to let Mimi and Dino handle him. She could live without talking to Ric. But she was also getting impatient at how slow Mimi and Dino were at handling this case. Why couldn't they just reveal the whole truth to the entire clan?

Claire was also weighed down by guilt whenever she was with her closest friends, especially Marc and Pia. She felt smaller, as though her inner self had crumbled and shrunk. She knew that having either Marc or Pia as a sounding board would have helped to ease her feeling of isolation. She did not want to carry around any secrets. She wanted her freedom badly. Freedom from guilt. She desperately needed someone to talk to about this.

#

Marc and Rinka finally arrived at their Amsterdam hotel on Friday. Claire huddled with the two at the lobby café while waiting for Marc's room to become available. She pointed at the ice dispenser in the hallway as though it were the eighth wonder of the world. 'Why oh why would they have this in the northern hemisphere. There's one on every floor too,' she said.

'Ah . . . you should read that ice cream article I saw in some journal,' Marc replied.

'What did it say?' Claire was curious.

'Apparently in some markets, ice cream knows no season. Consumption level stays pretty much the same throughout the year,' Marc shared.

'That's possible. I've seen kids eating slushies during theatre intermissions at West End. Even in winter,' Claire said.

'You should come to Japan and try every ice cream flavour imaginable,' Rinka said.

'Now I'm feeling cold all of a sudden. We better stop this talk of ice cream before I freeze,' Marc pretended to shiver.

'We must try some ice cream on this trip, Marc,' Rinka begged.

'Why not?' he shrugged.

In the evening, they took a cab to a design café at Westerpark, which seemed to be quiet initially but was soon filled with their voices. Over drinks, they dissected each other's so-called love life or the lack of it.

'That's the one thing that bonds us together, we are all single, and don't seem to have any prospects on the horizon,' Rinka said.

'Speak for yourself,' Marc laughed.

'Marc, have you been hiding something or someone?' Rinka was intrigued.

'I can't talk details now, but yes, I think I finally found my O.N.E.,' he said.

'How and when did this happen? Why am I hearing about it only now?' Claire sat up straight.

'Claire, do you remember Steve, my roommate at Holland Village?' Marc said.

'Yes, of course, the neat-freak guy,' Claire was feeling incredulous.

'Precisely. That time we shared the house with Jen, who, as you know, is a space-hogger like me. I think Steve couldn't adjust to our chaos so he got his own place after a few months,' Marc paused to take a sip of his wine.

'So then, how did you, two, happen?' Claire asked.

'I bumped into him in one of those wine and cheese events at Robertson Quay. Away from our cluttered former home, we seemed to be better versions of ourselves. To make a long story short, we hit it off and have been going out since then.'

'I want to hear the details. Like how many dates did you have before you decided to be official, you know,' Rinka leaned forward.

'That's enough shocker for the day, Rinks,' Marc smiled. 'Now, let's talk about you, and you,' he looked expectantly at Claire.

Claire also had many questions, but she understood Marc's need for discretion out of deference to Steve who worked for a traditional corporation. Up until now, it never occurred to Claire that Marc would be in a serious relationship. After all he was the one who had told her several times that he was in no rush, having suffered a traumatic break-up from his last relationship.

The next morning Claire and Marc met at breakfast while Rinka slept in claiming she was not a breakfast person anyway.

'When are you moving in with him?' Claire asked.

'Early next year,' Marc replied.

'That's not too far away,' Claire's eyes widened.

'It's rather whirlwind, I know, but I feel that moving in is the right thing to do. Anyways, enough about me. We haven't gotten around to talking about you,' Marc said in a more sombre tone.

'I've told you about my whole story,' she replied, rearranging the napkin on her lap.

'Haven't you met someone new, like more recently, the present time, as in this month for example?' he asked.

'You've seen my schedule, no? Do you think I have the time to meet Prince Charming when I've been running from one pitch to another?' she complained.

'What about the weekends when we're not together?'

'Like I have so many. Well, definitely not the last one as I was busy correcting some goddamn errors,' she said.

'What about back in Singapore?' he asked.

'If only Pia were a guy,' she replied.

'What about the up and coming politicians in the Philippines? Don't you know a couple of heirs to the political thrones?'

'I hate politicians to Pluto and back. You already know that. Not that there are any interesting ones anyway.' She had met some who unabashedly admired her. She hated the tribe and their corny pickup lines. In fact hate was too mild a word to describe how she felt about them. Loathe was a better word. She started frowning at the thought.

'I'm only asking, Claire. No harm intended,' his voice trailed off.

'The more we're talking about this, the more I realize that my life in the past five years has solely been about this job that eats into all my waking hours,' she said. For some reason she could not stop bellyaching and at breakfast too.

'Don't be testy now. I know you're grumpy in the mornings, but I haven't seen you this grumpy.'

'Sorry. It's true, though, that I hardly have time for myself. The travels have become more ridiculous. One day I'm in Guangzhou and the next day, in Geneva. So, yes, even if, let's say, I have the time to go to bars after work, I don't think I stay in any given city long enough to meet Mr Right.'

'First of all, you are far from a bar crawler. I know how much you cringe when you're in a crowded elevator even if you've tried to hide that from others. Being in a bar by yourself? That would be the day, or late night,' Marc said, as he poured more coffee into her cup before refilling his.

She started feeling self-conscious though she should not be, this being Marc after all. She could be herself with him.

Marc arched one eyebrow enquiringly when she remained quiet. 'Cat got your tongue?' he asked. 'What a rare occasion!'

'I'm just weirded out,' she said.

'That I asked a banal question?'

'No, it's far from banal. I know some women live for marriage prospects. There's nothing wrong with that. I'm not going to make any judgement. Who am I to do so, right? In any case this whole conversation has got me thinking harder. Could it be that I'm doing it all wrong, that I'm too uptight?' she said.

'You're definitely more neurotic than most women I know, but please elaborate on what you mean when you say uptight,' he asked, his thick brows now merging into a uni-brow as he frowned.

'I should stop overanalysing every single thing before anything could even happen. I should go out more and be more relaxed around guys,' she declared.

'I'm all for transformation. But that doesn't sound like the kind of transformation I like. You make it sound so not you,' he frowned.

'I really should try to be more *outgoing*. You know what I mean, just go out and have fun, with low or no expectations,' she said.

'Who are you likely to meet in those bars? Let me tell you this. You will meet guys who have one clear objective. I don't need to spell that out for you. They won't even bother to wake beside you the morning after. Low expectations indeed,' he said, putting his cup down with a thud.

'That's taking it to another extreme. I don't think I can do one-night stands,' Claire cringed visibly at the mere thought of it.

'Claire, I will say this only once, so you better listen. You are decent, intelligent, and accomplished. So don't ever sell yourself short. Attractive does not even begin to describe you. But you also have this thick air of aloofness. Dear girl, it scares the hell out of guys. On the other hand, it's probably an effective screener. At least it can protect you from wimps,' he went on.

'I almost ended up with one, remember?' she said trying to smile now.

'That one was more slimeball than wimp. Oh that's another category to steer away from. Oh please, don't remind me,' he rolled his eyes.

'This kind of discussion does not go well with breakfast. Topic change. So what's the agenda for the day?' she asked.

'Have you forgotten? You said we could check out the museum district—*there's Rikjs, Van Gogh, and the design museum right beside it*,' Marc tried to mimic her.

#

Claire soon found Marc taking in every detail of Rembrandt's *Night Watch*. It took effort to tear him away and lead him to Vermeer's *The Milkmaid*. 'Now, here's another masterpiece, and my all-time favourite so far,' she said.

'How did it become a masterpiece, it's so tiny,' Marc said.

'Yeah, but do you realize that this lady here is more noble than those queens and other royals in giant canvasses.' For Claire, *The Milkmaid* spoke greater volumes than bigger and more famous paintings. She would have *The Milkmaid* over *Mona Lisa* any time of day. It was also more meaningful than many gigantic murals like Picasso's *Guernica* for example. She hated highly politicized paintings especially when the artist had questionable politics. More than that, she wanted a piece of art to be pleasing and to enlighten rather than to incite or evoke anger. She tried to get Marc to see her point of view but then she knew she had lost Marc's attention after the *Night Watch*. She remembered Melanie saying that she adored the *Rijks* more than other major museums. Though Melanie admired Van Gogh the most, she was equally knowledgeable about Vermeer. She remembered how animated Melanie was when talking about artists and their works and how she had enhanced Claire's museum visits with her insights.

Claire and Marc practically breezed through the other sections of the museum. However much Claire wanted to linger in some sections Marc counteracted with an equally stronger tug to make her move faster. Meanwhile Rinka was elsewhere taking photos with her bulky camera. They regrouped after an hour and went to Dam Square for some shopping and walked some more until they had reached Spui and decided to go into one of the oldest brown cafés in the area. The dark wall inside transported Claire back in time and she was awestruck by the whole atmosphere and would have stayed there longer had there been a space inside or even upstairs. Eventually they found a table in the porch, not the best of places given the weather, but it was covered with transparent plastic sheeting for winter and the area allowed them a view of the pedestrians. A group of youngsters beside their table were laughing infectiously and even offered Claire's group a taste of the brownie that they were passing around. Marc smiled and declined politely knowing only too well what was included in the brownie.

The three of them had been working for some time now, but travelling together like this made Claire realize some of the quirks of her colleagues for the first time, including the fact that Marc could easily lose his temper when badly in need of his caffeine fix. He was almost rude to the shop assistant at the boutique when the latter took time and came back with the news that Marc's jeans size was not available. While Marc could burst into tempers when stressed, Rinka's quirks were more physiological. Rinka slept like a log. This would have been good news as it gave Claire time to read before bedtime or upon waking up, but Rinka also snored, especially when she was physically exhausted. This tended to awaken Claire, a light sleeper, in the middle of the night.

The next day, Rinka went to Paris for her 'much-needed' shopping while Claire and Marc stayed for the pitch presentation. In between presentation rehearsals, Claire and Marc would check out nearby coffee shops and just hang out there while waiting for their next call. They even checked out the inner streets at Jordaan—weirdly, in search of ice cream, even in this cold weather and when Rinka was no longer there to remind them. They both tried the speculoos flavour that their colleagues had recommended. Marc relished his ice cream, but Claire did not enjoy it as much. The longer she was with Marc, the guiltier she felt about hiding her situation from him. She was on the verge of pouring out all her secrets. But perhaps now was not the time, when Marc was having utmost pleasure with his *speculoos* ice cream.

After dinner that Monday, Claire finally gathered the courage to reveal the latest about her identity: 'You're the only one I've told this to so far. I'd wanted to tell you this ever since I discovered it, but I never had the guts until now. I've been feeling guiltier the longer I held it from you. I could not even enjoy that speculoos ice cream,' she laughed at the thought. 'But now I feel so much better. I'm simply being me. I've got nothing else to hide. What you see is what you get. No longer an iceberg,' she heaved a sigh of relief.

'I'm here for you, Claire. I only wish you had told me earlier so that you didn't have to carry this guilt around. It's easy to assume everything is normal with you. You don't seem to get hassled easily,' Marc said, leaning forward to look at Claire's eye bags, 'Or maybe you're just good at "concealing" it,' he added.

'You're right. I've been applying extra layers of concealer these days,' she chuckled.

'You've mastered the art of concealing,' Mark smiled.

'You know what they say about necessity. I've been waking up in the middle of the night the past few weeks. It's too ironic, isn't it? I'm a congressman's daughter after all, for all my hatred of politicians,' she said.

'It's not your fault to begin with. I wish it didn't affect you this way. I don't want you to get sick,' he said. 'Your uncle slash father doesn't yet know that you've uncovered this big secret, right? So let it be. Why are you taking it upon yourself to correct every wrong situation? To borrow Billy Joel's words, you did not start the fire,' Marc added.

'It's unfortunate, though, that I'm a product of that mess,' Claire replied.

'Don't get into the self-pity zone. It's indeed unfortunate that it happened and that it happened to you, of all people. But it doesn't change you, Claire. You are your own person, no matter who your biological parents are. You are an achiever in your own right. You don't need your relatives for validation,' Marc tried to reassure her.

'How could I hold myself up if I'm so ashamed of my biological roots, if the blood running in my very own veins is from someone I loathe,' she tried to hold off tears that gathered in her eyes.

'You are a different person from your biological parents. You might share their DNA but, for God's sake, you are nothing like them,' Marc went to her side, shaking his head in frustration. He cupped her head between his hands, lifted her chin and stared deeply into her eyes. 'Claire. You are a beautiful person inside and out. Don't let this episode change you, or your course.' Marc wouldn't let go of her until after she nodded. He wiped her tears away and hugged her gently. When he thought she had stopped crying, he pulled her up. 'Come, let's go. I think it's been too much of a week for us.' He helped her out of her seat. 'In this theatre called life, I don't think we are meant for drama. It's not our genre,' he said solemnly.

When they reached their hotel lobby, Marc lifted her chin, 'I would love to see you to your room, but you know the rules, right? You reminded me about it once. But if it gets too unbearable, call me any time,' he said as he ushered her to the lift. 'I'll take you back to that ice cream shop tomorrow,' he added.

Claire nodded and hugged him tight. Now she could be with Marc with a much clearer conscience and that made a vast difference in her mood.

'Oh wait, Josh is swinging by for the day tomorrow. He's in Paris for work and just found out that I'm currently here,' he said.

'It's okay. We can have the ice cream some other day. I'll be fine,' she said.

'No, what I mean is, could I ask him to join us?' Marc asked.

'It's more I rather than he who's tagging along,' she replied.

'Oh Claire, I don't know any more who comes first between you and my brother. Anyways, he's generally self-sufficient, as you might have noticed last time,' Marc said, 'especially around food,' he added.

'Marc,' Claire reminded him to be nice.

'It's true though,' he said.

'Please. Josh is a fun conversationalist. We spent an entire afternoon at Toast Box, remember?' Claire asked.

'Oh yes, I've forgotten how you two quickly got along so well after that dinner at Prego. Well, Josh loves to talk, especially about books, which I assume is pretty much what you talked about,' he replied.

'There was that. He's also conversant on other topics as you would know. You were the one who suggested I call him up to get his "expert" opinion about the emerging trend on entertainment on-demand.'

'Nerds of the same feather . . .' he said, rolling his eyes teasingly.

#

The next day Claire went back to the speculoos ice-cream shop with Marc and Josh. Claire was more relaxed now that her burden of hiding something from Marc had been lifted, so she could savour her ice cream. 'Wow! This is more zen than anything,' Claire said.

'What are you talking about?' Marc asked.

'Josh devouring his ice cream to the exclusion of all else,' Claire said.

'Oh yeah. That's his religion. And all other food items too,' Marc shrugged.

'Why are you guys so jealous of my mindfulness? Can I help it if I'm more enlightened than the two of you combined?' Josh said, licking the last bit of his ice cream with relish.

They proceeded to Dam Square, yet again, but this time they looked at other shops where Marc could possibly purchase a new pair of jeans. While Marc was busy in the fitting room, Josh amused Claire with his made-up stories about the three mannequins by the display window. He invented three different personas for the three mannequins, Andre, Balzac and Casper.

'But Balzac is French and Casper is a ghost, so that leaves just Andre with a credible story' Claire laughed.

'Oh please, let's just pretend for a moment that Balzac is a Dutch baker here, and Casper is the CEO of a giant conglomerate,' he said.

Soon Marc was back with a shopping bag and a big smile, too, glad that his shopping mission was finally accomplished. But then he remembered that Josh had to leave soon. 'Oh why do you have to go back so soon, Josh?' he asked on their way out to the taxi stand.

'It's a work trip, Marc. I've enjoyed this day-off with you and Claire, but now I gotta get back to Paris and earn my fee,' he said looking serious now too. 'I hate goodbyes,' he said hugging them both, before getting into his cab.

Marc and Claire then hailed another cab to return to their hotel. Both were unusually silent on the ride as though suddenly drained of all energy.

13

Santa Rosa, Valle Viejo

The Christmas Eve celebration at the Rosales House went off without a glitch and with less crying than the previous year. The party at the farm was even grander than before. But the days around Christmas had become more subdued for the grown-ups. Increasingly the holiday was becoming an affair that they celebrated more for the sake of the next generation, Mike's and JM's kids, who were largely oblivious to the undercurrents in the house. The kids were preoccupied with their games as usual, egging on the grown-ups to chase them around. Claire was absent-mindedly following their antics one afternoon when Mimi came to sit beside her.

'Claire, I'm dying to hear the latest,' Mimi whispered.

'We can talk about it tomorrow. Could we go to the farm in the morning? I also have a few questions I've been wanting to ask you,' Claire replied.

Mimi nodded, quickly changing the topic and pretending to talk about shopping upon seeing that Cecille, carrying a platter of sweets and chocolates, was approaching.

Ric joined the clan only during dinner and kept checking his watch throughout; he even skipped dessert. He excused himself to join his aides at the pavilion-like gazebo behind the house. The place had its own bar, a barbecue pit, a kitchenette, and gaming tables, as well as its own music system, where the aides played old country songs on loud volume. Earlier, Claire could not understand why the aides would be hanging around all night when they should be with their families. She found out from Cecille that they worked in shifts. Claire could hear their boisterous laughter periodically. When Gloria was still alive, she did not tolerate this level of noise, but now it seemed to have become the norm. It was partly because of this that Claire chose not to stay late in the house especially as the gazebo was within earshot of the room that she usually occupied.

Back at their family home, Claire enjoyed the post-dinner moments with Dino and Anna in their drawing room. Dino put on a Frank Sinatra record before reclining on his chair nearby. When Remy came to ask what drink she would have, Claire opted for hot chocolate, something that reminded her of childhood. The sweater weather now and the Christmas songs playing softly in the background were conducive to full-blown reminiscing. Dino reminded her of how she had made a pile of snow from soapsuds one Christmas season.

'It was Mama who taught me how to make it. But why, in the first place, did I want snow in a tropical country? It was probably the influence of all the Christmas jingles I've been listening to,' she laughed at her childhood ignorance.

Anna sat next to her on the three-seater sofa. 'I've been talking to your Daddy about opening a café,' she told Claire.

'That sounds interesting, Mama,' she said tucking her feet under her as she sat cross-legged facing Anna. 'But don't you have your hands full, especially with Buena Vista?' Claire was sceptical.

'I'm usually done with Buena Vista-related work by lunchtime and I'm mostly free in the afternoons. Also, this is going to be a joint effort with your Auntie Beth so it won't be very time-consuming for me,' Anna explained.

'But isn't a café difficult to manage, specially with the dinner crowd? They can get rowdy,' Claire said.

'We're thinking more of a bakery, pastry and coffee shop.'

'Whoa, coffee shop! Yes, this town definitely needs a decent one. I'll be your number-one supporter,' she smiled excitedly. 'Daddy, what say you?' Claire asked.

'Do you think I haven't heard enough about this project proposal? Your Mama and Auntie Beth have been pestering me a lot about this over the past few months,' Dino replied. Though he used the word 'pestering', Claire knew from his smile that he did not oppose the idea.

'We can hire some of the farmers' wives and train them to be bakers. I thought that could contribute to their income,' Anna added.

'That sounds truly wonderful, Ma. I never thought of it as an opportunity to help the village women. That makes it an even greater venture.'

'I think I know where this conversation is heading to,' Dino said, as he pulled out magazines from the rack and started reading articles about farming and gardening.

It was almost dawn when Claire and Anna concluded their chat about the café. Claire's last thought before finally drifting off to sleep was how proud she was of Anna for thinking of ways to help other women.

#

Buena Vista

The next day Mimi picked Claire up on the way to the farm. Ed, ever-prepared, was already waiting by the brick steps. Upon Mimi's request, Ed took them around the garden first before ushering them to the house. Mimi and Claire settled on their favourite spot on the porch area overlooking the cathedral. Lorna brought a pot of freshly brewed coffee, *pan de sal* with white cheese, butter, and sardines on the side, and native rice cakes. When the helper was out of earshot, Mimi pushed her sunglasses up to her hair before asking about Melanie. 'When are you planning to meet her family?' she asked.

'I don't know yet, Auntie. Maybe at the next New York City marathon. Or Thanksgiving. Or maybe when they come to Asia,' she replied.

'At least now you know where to find her,' Mimi said.

'She seems to have a wholesome family.'

'I've never met her, but I remember from Mama's accounts that she was truly smart.'

'She does look smart and wouldn't have done well if she weren't,' Claire said, surprised that she was feeling somewhat proud as she said this. She held her coffee mug and luxuriated in its aroma before finally taking a sip. She had forgotten how good their local brew tasted.

'As for the task assigned to me on this, I'm having dinner with Ric tonight,' Mimi sighed. 'I wish Mama were still here. She would know how to handle this situation.'

'Auntie, I wish I had discovered this secret earlier,' Claire put her cup down. 'Learning about it this late makes it doubly awkward for me. I hate that I could not even talk about it with my cousins,' she snapped.

'I understand and I'm really sorry you're suffering because of all these. I wish I could do more and resolve this issue soonest,' Mimi said, reaching out to hold Claire's hand.

'The worst part is, I did not even have a hand in the situation. I'm suffering because of another person's immaturity and immorality,' she sighed. 'I wonder how you reacted to this the first time you had heard about it,' Claire voiced out her frustration.

'I did not speak to Ric for a long time back then. It was a tumultuous and completely draining period. But Mama had said that we couldn't choose our family. We could only try to make the best of our relations. She had emphasized at every chance that it was my responsibility to shine some light whenever and wherever it was needed,' Mimi said. 'I also realized I could not keep on blaming him for a situation that gave you to us. You were a far greater blessing than he was a nuisance. Having you around helped to heal the wounds,' she added.

'He still needs to be told of the current situation. He must own up to his mistakes.'

'Yes, it's important to tell the truth, but it's also more important to tell it at the right time, especially if this truth can trigger another catastrophe,' Mimi said softly, putting her cup down.

'What am I supposed to do in the meantime? How do you think I feel every time I look at my cousins and I'm reminded that they are in fact my half-brothers? How do you think I feel each time I look at Uncle Ric and still find it hard to believe, or accept, that he is my biological father,' Claire stood up and paced around the porch.

Mimi was almost too shocked to say anything. She got up and put her arms around Claire.

'Didn't anyone have a clue? Didn't anyone suspect that Mama could not really have been pregnant at that time? Didn't Mama tell anyone like her closest confidante, or Auntie Beth, that I am not really her daughter?'

'I'm sorry to say this, Claire, but your Lola, for all her velvet gloves and gentleness, was a smooth operator,' Mimi shook her head. 'She had asked everyone, including Anna, to sign a confidentiality contract. Knowing Anna, she would have been too scared to tell anyone, even her own parents, had they still been alive. Besides, they lived in Mindanao and were too far from everything.'

'What if Mama starts talking now?'

'I doubt it. The people here don't care as much any more. Anna wouldn't want to rock the boat, more so now that she is used to this life for more than thirty years now. Besides, in her own way, she cares about you a lot. She wouldn't want to hurt you. Nobody would want to do that,' Mimi added.

'Why can't we just lay it on the line at least within the family?'

'This decision is not up to me. I don't know the dynamics between Ric and Cecille. It seems like their issues are getting worse. I'm finding it awkward to stay at the main house whenever I come for a visit. They bicker too much.'

'And do I keep on holding my breath until somebody is brave enough to tell the truth?'

'I don't want to sugar-coat it, but that's exactly how things should be for now. Election is coming up, as you know. In fact, Melanie was not supposed to let anyone in on this. Unless the contract she signed had a domicile limitation, making it valid only in the Philippines. Who would have predicted that Melanie would be making it to the US like that? That's one thing your Lola, in all her smartness, had not foreseen.'

#

Place of Pilgrimage

Mimi led the Rosales women on a pilgrimage to a religious site two hours away from Valle Viejo. Inside the church, the party gathered at the stations of the cross and they prayed the rosary at each stop. It had not occurred to Claire that they would be continuing with this tradition of regularly visiting religious places after Gloria's death, but increasingly, Mimi had taken on this aspect, organizing a pilgrimage for the clan every time she returned to Valle Viejo.

Claire joined the group at the first station of the cross and after that she decided to sit in one of the pews at the back. She did not want to follow the group blindly and preferred to pray in her own way and with her personal intentions. She stepped out to the small garden from across the church, which stood majestically on top of a hill. It provided a view of the valley below including Valle Viejo. Claire could see the river winding down the hills and the lush green trees along its banks. On the far side of the bank, steps were carved out of boulders leading to one of the larger cave complexes in the valley. She recalled having gone inside it during a school trip. It was dark inside as in other caves, but there was a hole above the biggest chamber from where daylight could stream in. Sometimes the light would reflect on the stalagmites and stalactites making the area less eerie than the rest. At the end of the tunnel, there were boats waiting for visitors who wanted to go white-water rafting along the most rugged stretch of the river. She was too young to try white-water rafting then, but now that she was old enough, she did not find it thrilling any more. Or perhaps, she simply did not have the courage. She had not tried any extreme sports apart from parasailing over the waters of Jimbaran Bay in Bali, if that could be considered extreme enough.

Mimi joined Claire at the garden some time later. She looked around to check if there was anyone else from their party. When she was sure there was no one else, she asked Claire if they could go for a short walk a bit farther from the church. 'I've finally had a chance to talk to your uncle,' Mimi whispered.

'What did he say?' Claire asked.

'He said this was not the right time because of the upcoming elections yet again. He also said something about Cecille, which I didn't quite understand. But the main message is, this is not the right time to talk to him.'

Claire nodded. Whatever remaining respect she had for Ric was further eroded and it had now dropped to ground level or plummeted even lower. He pretended to be a fearless patriarch but was, in fact, the biggest coward she had ever met.

'He was surprised you managed to find Melanie. He said he had forgotten about her. Just between the two of us, I think he is scared at what else could possibly happen,' Mimi whispered.

'He should have been scared this whole time. I wonder how he manages to sleep at night,' Claire said.

'We must plan our action properly. I know this is tough for you, but we have to consider the bigger picture, how this could impact the whole family. I hate to see the Rosales clan facing more threats. I can't bear skeletons coming out of the closet.'

'Look, Auntie, I don't mean to be insensitive especially to you and Daddy, but I still believe in this old cliché that only the truth can set us all free. Clearly the ball is in Uncle Ric's court and until he does something, we can never have peace of mind,' Claire replied.

'I feel as though I don't know him any more. He's acting like a total stranger. At least when we were kids, he would still listen to me or Dino.'

'How did he become like this?'

'I suppose Papa was partly to blame for his odd way of parenting. He used to punish Dino and Ric a lot. Shouting. Spanking. Shaming. You name it, he had done it.'

'Punish for what?'

'It could be over the simplest of things. He gave them unreasonable tasks like cutting grass at the farm at the height of summer or cleaning the toilets at the municipal office just to show his people that nothing was beneath his boys. If they missed out on the slightest of things, the quantum of punishment was too much, hardly commensurate with the sin.'

'Didn't Lola have a say in all that?'

'It was a different era back then. The guys needed to show how tough they were. Papa used to punish the boys in public to prove his impartiality. He even tied Ric to a banana trunk all day, like a monkey in the zoo, for everyone to see. And for what? For unintentionally breaking one of his golf tournament trophies in the library?' Mimi was breathing hard in agitation.

'I've heard about his being tough and all, but not in this way,' Claire gasped in disbelief.

'Consider yourself fortunate not to have known him. Our brokenness, in one way or another, was largely or partly because of what he did. I would cry and hide behind Mama's skirt every time I heard the boys wailing. I hate to blame anyone else for the choices I've made as an adult, but my psychotherapist had told me long ago that this childhood trauma probably contributed to my decision of not having children of my own,' Mimi said.

'Auntie, I didn't know all this. I'm sorry,' Claire was taken aback by this information.

'It's okay, I came to terms with it eventually. It was clearly too late by then, but I guess that's my fate. Besides, I consider you and your cousins as my own, so in that sense I'm not totally childless,' Mimi opened her arms to hug her.

'Oh, Auntie Mimi,' Claire could not help but hug her tight.

'As for Dino, he withdrew into himself. On the other hand, I think Ric had become desensitized to pain,' Mimi said almost cruelly.

'So desensitized that he has become the inflictor,' Claire said disentangling herself from Mimi.

'Lately I'm seeing more and more of Ric's cruelty, which to me is a sign of weakness. To mask his cowardice. Maybe that's why he needs to rely so much on Cecille when it comes to politics and to winning the next election,' she said.

Claire could only shake her head at the mention of how cruel Ric was.

'Please be patient. We'll figure something out. I can't handle any more crises at this point.' Mimi's shoulders drooped, her eyes seemed to be pleading.

'Of course, Auntie. While I'm impatient at how slow things are, I'm sensitive enough not to do anything rash or radical. You must know that.'

'Sometimes I can't be too sure about that. Increasingly, I see signs of your grit. It reminds me of Mama when she would fight Papa back. You resemble her in that department, and like her, your gentle bearing can be deceptive,' Mimi said in a much softer voice seeing that Cecille was pulling away from the crowd and was coming in their direction.

'I'm not sure I like this comparison with Lola. But yes, I'll be quiet, Auntie. Only for now. I can't be quiet forever. So let's resolve this sooner.'

Mimi squeezed Claire's hand before turning to smile at Cecille who was now showing a bunch of rosary beads she had bought from the shop beside the chapel.

#

Santa Rosa, Valle Viejo

Claire felt like an imposter during the remainder of the holiday, discovering so much about the past and yet pretending that everything was as it used to be. She successfully avoided any encounter with Ric, which was not that difficult, as she had hardly interacted with him even in the past anyway. She consciously tried to be good company and put on a happy face in the presence of her cousins and their families.

Ric's immediate family was busy strategizing for the upcoming elections. In addition to Ric's re-election bid, Mike was also running for the mayoralty of Santa Rosa while Cecille was aiming for a place in the provincial board. Even JM who typically shied away from politics grew enthusiastic about Mike's candidacy. He went out of his way to meet more people and to help lay the groundwork for Mike, to borrow his parlance.

'You should come home in May,' JM said, while they were catching up in the family room at the Rosales House, watching over the kids, who did not need much watching over anyway as they were busy with their new toys.

'I would like to, especially for Mike, but I can't promise at this point,' she replied.

'Hmmm, I think I know the reason. Could it be too much work again?' JM tried to tease her.

'They simply pile up non-stop. I'm starting to feel like a loser,' she shook her head.

'You've again been travelling a lot too. Every time I call, you're in one city or another.'

'Yep, that's my life,' she nodded. 'In any case, it goes without saying that I'll help in the election as much as I can. With the Internet and all the new technology available, I'm sure I can do more things than before without having to be here.'

'Yes, that's right, but I'm sure everyone would feel better if you could be here physically. Look at Auntie Mimi. It's no secret that she's averse to all the chaos during elections but she has promised to be here in May nonetheless,' JM paused. 'We need her for Daddy's sake more than anyone's,' he added.

'What do you mean?'

'She doesn't need to be here for Mike who is a sure bet from what I hear. Mummy has been doing such a great job all these years that the townsfolk are totally devoted to her. Her endorsement of

Mike practically equates to victory. Mummy herself has more than the requisite votes for board membership,' JM explained.

'And Uncle Ric?' she asked.

'Daddy's is a different story. I mean we'll always have Santa Rosa, but we need to be stronger outside of our bailiwick to ensure victory. His opponents seem to have strengthened since the last round. They seem to be using guerrilla tactics, building strength in far-flung places that Daddy has not covered regularly,' JM explained.

'Why, what happened? Why wasn't he covering all the towns in his district?' Claire's eyes widened in disbelief. 'That's unfair to the constituents in those areas,'

'He has been spending more time in Manila ever since Lola passed away. Frankly, we don't know how to manage without Lola,' JM sighed.

'This sounds more serious than I thought,' Claire said.

'This is beyond even Mummy. They've been arguing a lot because he does not listen to her. The congressional election is a bigger game and this time we have more vicious opponents. I wish we were a bigger clan,' JM said.

Claire wondered if these issues had already existed and that perhaps she, being too wrapped up in her own world, had simply been oblivious to it all. 'It does sound like we really need Auntie Mimi more than ever. We're lucky that their real estate business gives her flexibility to spend more time here,' she said.

'We're lucky to have Uncle Paul, too, who understands the situation, even if he himself could not make it on some of the trips,' JM said, referring to Mimi's husband. 'He's a close friend of the governor, as you know; the governor's family always stay at their place whenever they are in San Francisco,' JM added. 'The only good news so far is that the governor's influence is ever growing.'

14

Santa Rosa, Valle Viejo

The campaign period in Santa Rosa was more celebratory than contentious with most townsfolk committing their support for Mike as mayor even months prior to election. There was a fiesta feel to the events with sorties turning out to be like get-togethers rather than traditional campaigns that tried to persuade or change voters' opinion. Various gatherings became venues for consolidating Mike's supporters. Claire did not need to be in Santa Rosa for this. She could simply contribute to Mike's campaign funds and help to buy more umbrellas and other items for his supporters.

It was a whole different story for Ric's congressional bid. Ric's opponent, Arthur Fernandez, apparently received huge funding from a national sponsor and he had been spending lavishly, giving away mobile-phone cards, instant-noodle pouches, sacks of rice, and every imaginable good, and even cash to the electorate. Claire looked at the results of the monthly pre-survey, that JM had sent earlier, and it showed Fernandez's voter share on a sustained uptrend. In the latest read, he trailed Ric only by the slightest of margins. With a consistent growth rate and a little more push, Fernandez, former mayor of a logging town, could soon match Ric neck and neck. Claire now understood the gravity of JM's call an hour ago. She could hear panic in his voice. He needed her there at

Valle Viejo and begged her to come. It was rare for JM to beg her for anything.

Even Mimi was soon on the phone. '*Hija*, please set aside any grudges for now,' she said.

'Auntie, please, I've been very patient for the longest time,' Claire replied.

'We have to unite now more than ever. Your uncle needs to win. You know very well that the survival of our clan depends on it,' Mimi said.

'But it doesn't make things right,' Claire sighed.

'The Rosales blood runs in your veins, too, *hija*. So please, do your best to help.'

Claire would not do it for Ric even if he begged her to do so. On the other hand, she was a Rosales too. Her relatives asked her to be there for the clan, more than for Ric. They all needed to do more than their usual share to compensate for Gloria's absence. In past elections, Gloria had always been stumping for Ric, something she had done all her life, having grown up in a political clan herself and having eventually married into one. She used to lead non-government organizations or NGOs for women and marginalized townsfolk that helped them in starting small businesses or further their children's education. In return many of the townsfolk were always grateful to and revered Gloria a lot. But since Gloria's death, the NGOs's leadership had been gradually passed on to the governor's family, which in turn helped to grow the governor's popularity. Over time, the Rosales's interaction with the womenfolk was reduced dramatically as Mimi spent most of her time in the United States, while Cecille focused solely on Santa Rosa. Claire discovered this disturbing situation during her call with JM and Mimi.

#

Mimi arrived at Valle Viejo a few weeks before the election, helping to manage the inner circle of staff that was responsible for directing the bigger events and the overall campaign strategy. She also visited women's organizations and parents' associations, while Ric, JM and Mike covered far-flung villages.

Even Dino actively reached out to farmers and engaged with the leaders of their associations and cooperatives. This must have been a strain for Dino who was more introverted and preferred to connect in less-crowded settings. Apparently, Dino became aware of the district's eroding support for Ric ahead of the other family members. He had flagged this up to Ric much earlier, but Ric had simply ignored him.

JM was on the phone again the next day. 'Claire, I wouldn't ask you this if the situation weren't dire,' he said.

'I understand JM, but I haven't heard anything from Uncle Ric,' Claire said.

'Daddy is not in the right frame of mind. Even if he were, he wouldn't normally ask the younger generation a favour. You know how proud he is.'

'Look JM, if it were for you, I wouldn't need to think twice. I'd be there right away.'

'Whatever your beef with Daddy is, please set it aside for now. Come home for my sake. Come home for the sake of the clan,' he begged.

Claire knew that JM had assumed her hesitation was due to some trivial reason, but she could not divulge the real reason on the phone. 'Let me talk to my manager tomorrow and find out if they can let me off for a few days,' she gave in finally.

'Thank you. This is one of those times I blame myself for migrating. In a way it's a sign of cowardice. I should have remained home and worked harder to strengthen our standing in Valle Viejo,' he sighed.

'JM, please. This is not your sole responsibility. You can't change things single-handedly. Obviously, Uncle Ric has to work the hardest being the standard bearer. He is the congressman. Not you. Or me. We can prop him up, but only to a certain point. The rest is up to him,' she said.

'I know. But still, things would have been better if we were all together. Here,' he said.

#

When Claire arrived in Santa Rosa, the Rosales compound was crowded and every corner was bursting with activities. The high walls were plastered with campaign posters, mostly for Ric. There were just a few reminders for Mike and Cecille. She had forgotten how crazy election seasons were in Santa Rosa in particular and Valle Viejo in general, having been away during the last three election cycles.

Campaign posters were far more sophisticated than Claire remembered. Even the radio ads and jingles were a riff of contemporary pop songs rather than regional folk songs. The surveys alone had become complex. In the past, the Rosales's could manage with just two pre-election surveys. Now they had a monthly read since January, and in the last two months they added weekly reads as well. While the campaign had a team dedicated to analysing the data, the family defaulted to getting Claire's analysis as well. In the past, her inputs were used mainly for confirmation, but now, it seemed everybody waited for her pronouncement before deciding on the next move.

On her way to the Rosales House, Claire smiled and nodded at the townsfolk milling about at the entrance even though she did not know any of them. Midway, Maritess came to usher her in. Inside, she found Anna, looking hassled and in the middle of giving instructions to the head cook. Claire hugged Anna who explained to her that she could help best in that capacity and she did not attempt to get into the so-called war-room discussions. Anna instructed Maritess to take Claire's luggage to her usual room and she herself led Claire to where the rest of the clan was waiting.

The inner part of the library was transformed into the war-room. While the campaign was headquartered in San Fernando, the clan held their most confidential meetings here, which usually involved only key family members and the most loyal aides. JM and Mimi were discussing charts and numbers on the large computer screen. Dino was reading some of the reports in a corner armchair. He immediately stood up to hug her. 'How was the drive, *hija*?' he asked.

'Smoother than I thought. Surprisingly there weren't too many traffic jams and detours. I suppose the government has rushed all the roadwork in time for elections,' she replied.

'Thank God, you're here finally,' JM practically lifted her as he hugged her tightly.

JM introduced the aide, who then excused himself to get some coffee.

'Claire, I'm so glad you're here. I don't know what to make of all these figures. It's much clearer when you explain things to me,' Mimi immediately launched, pointing at the screen and the printouts she was poring over.

'Let Claire catch her breath first, Auntie, I'm sure she didn't sleep on the drive,' JM reminded Mimi.

'I'm fine. I just need a cup of coffee. Mama is bringing it over,' Claire added, as apparently helpers were not allowed in the inner war-room. A guard even stood by the library entrance.

Later, Claire asked the group to huddle together so she could share her assessment based on the latest survey data: 'Uncle Ric has solid support here in Santa Rosa without a doubt. In San Fernando, they still remember Lola's father and his role as one of the city's modern-day founders. This residual support helps to lift the numbers,' Claire pointed at the figures. 'Now these are the towns where Uncle Ric has only marginal advantage. He needs to intensify his efforts there. On the other hand, these are the towns where he might lose substantially. But not all of these have to be given up easily. Maybe Santa Ana is a lost cause, that's Fernandez's hometown, isn't it? So, Uncle Ric should not waste any more time there. But in Zamora and Burgos, he has considerable support. He must tap into this base quickly to close the gap with Fernandez on the overall,' Claire explained.

'That makes a lot of sense,' JM nodded.

'Now, we need to check the events they've lined up here. Let's do some scenario playing. How would Fernandez's camp counteract? There could be several scenarios. We should be ready to respond accordingly.' Claire looked at her family for their reaction.

'That's precisely what I've been telling Ric,' Mimi said.

'We must understand voter sentiments here. We need a thorough understanding of what will move the needle. What motivates them? I don't think a simple song and dance would do the trick in these towns. We must do something really compelling,' Claire added.

The aide had been listening intently to Claire's explanation. Claire looked at him for possible inputs.

'Oh, Attorney Noel, how come you're unusually quiet? Have you known these all along?' JM asked.

'I've known some of these earlier, but not in this light I must admit. We haven't thought of prioritizing things this way or of giving up on Santa Ana completely. But, of course, Ma'am Claire is right. We must be more practical and prudent in allocating our resources given the limited time now. I need to rope in Leanne. She's in charge of the overall programming. Should we ask her to come over?' Noel asked.

'Let's wait for Daddy. He needs to listen to Claire's explanation. What time is he back?'

'He's supposed to be here at lunchtime,' Noel replied.

They took a break from the war-room and went for early lunch in the private dining room where they were soon joined by Ric, Cecille, and Mike.

After lunch, Claire found herself explaining things to Ric for the first time. 'These are the critical spots,' she repeated her earlier analysis for Ric and Cecille's benefit and as she did so, she could see both of them becoming more concerned and worried. 'We must review the events lined up for the coming days and prioritize our resources accordingly. By that, I don't mean just the campaign paraphernalia or whatever souvenirs your team is planning to distribute,' she said.

'What exactly can we do? Do you have any suggestions?' Ric asked the team.

When they remained quiet, Claire continued with her explanation. 'You have to be more visible, physically. If you could still manage it, buy more advertising spots on the radio.'

'Why radio?' Ric asked, frowning.

'Most farmers still listen to the radio especially in the morning before going to the farm, while in the farm, and again in the afternoon while taking a break. That's according to the media habits report,' she answered.

'Noel, could you show me the highlights of that report after this,' Ric said.

'Yes, sir,' Noel replied and went to pull out a thick report.

'What about the message?' Mimi raised her eyebrows.

'What do you think would compel voters in these critical towns? Do we have any kind of understanding?' Claire asked.

'We're not exactly new in this business, are we?' Ric replied.

Cecille placed a finger on her pursed lips to hush Ric. She turned to Claire and said, 'Claire, please go on. What's your suggestion?'

'For example, if the community is comprised predominantly of farmers, you need to highlight the programmes and bills you have authored that directly benefit them today. You must also remind them of any concrete projects you have sponsored. Irrigation? Road construction? Driers? Also get the Key Opinion Leaders or KOLs to be more active in endorsing you. Similarly, when you're talking to merchant groups, you must highlight any tax reduction that they're enjoying because of you. Talk about the greater convenience in the new public markets, and so on. It's more about tailoring your message to the audience.'

'We've been doing this all along,' Ric shook his head. 'You know, this is why I don't want to hire too many consultants. What's that saying about them: they ask for your watch to tell you the time,' he said sneeringly.

'Ric, please could we listen to what Claire has to say,' Cecille reminded him again.

'I'm not telling you the time, Uncle Ric. I'm assuming that it was the first thing that you checked, otherwise you don't have a right to be in this business. What I'm trying to do now is help you realize how you got into this situation, however late in the day that realization might be,' she said, looking at Ric dispassionately. Claire was incensed by Ric's earlier comments, but she kept her emotions in check. She tapped into her considerable experience of presenting to a hostile audience, like some of her clients who chose not to believe the data when it did not serve their purpose. With her clients, she could go about explaining the 'questionable' finding with equanimity and even smile at the end of each explanation.

'Claire, cut to the chase, and tell me something new, one thing I don't yet know,' he said, getting up from his chair.

'Ric, just listen to this one, this is important. Claire, please go ahead, *hija*,' Mimi who had been pacing the room stopped midway between Ric and Claire and stood there while waiting for Claire to resume.

'Even if you knew the time, you probably didn't realize that it doesn't mean the same to everyone,' she said. 'Going back to this,' she pointed at the projected screen. 'I'm sure you know this already, the fact that you're losing in some of the towns. But I'm not sure you know why. This could be because your message might not be reaching your audience, or perhaps it doesn't resonate with them. Here, look at this, it shows Fernandez's spending on the radio. He spends more than you do in these stations,' Claire showed him the report. 'Look at this, these voters don't remember any of the things you've done,' she gave him the next report.

'Hold on a second. How do you know that these figures are true? How sure are you that this data is not manufactured?' Ric stared hard at Claire as though daring her to look down.

'I've cross-validated with other sources and the results are consistent. The spending report, for example, is a reliable industry report, but I've nonetheless checked with another independent source. The voters' advertising recall is from your own survey and

I also got the same feedback from various news articles and social media buzz reports. There's such a thing as triangulating data and connecting the dots. All these data from different sources tell the same story,' Claire said with her chin up and looking steadily at Ric.

Ric was about to say something but changed his mind and turned instead to his assistant. 'Noel, how come I didn't see this before? Were you aware that Fernandez was outspending me at Bombo Radio?' he asked.

'No, sir. We came to know about this report only after Ma'am Claire had looked for it,' Noel squirmed in his chair.

It was the first time that her relatives saw Claire in this mode. All these years Claire had been providing insights and strategy to many companies globally, but her own family was truly benefitting from her professional expertise only now. She could see the change in the expression of her parents, aunts, cousins, and even Ric, as she explained how one compelling event could tilt the votes to the opponent. Time was not on their side. Claire knew that she should not rock the boat now, so she only gave recommendations that would enhance existing game plans rather than make the team redraw the entire strategy.

Claire spent most of her days in the war-room while her relatives attended one campaign sortie after another. She helped the communications team to manage field reports that kept on coming every half-hour, guided them in encoding the data, and updated the scenarios they had created earlier.

At times, when Claire felt disoriented in the war-room, she would step out and go to her room upstairs where she would make a call to either Marc or Pia. Talking to either of them while in the thick of the election activities reminded her that she had her own neat world back in Singapore. There was too much pressure and too many people to please here. Claire and her relatives were all forced to smile even when townsfolk were blatantly taking advantage of their situation. Various charity groups kept on coming and asking for donations. In the Rosales's compound, Claire could not understand how the crowd automatically thickened during mealtimes. The kitchen must be a total mess with the non-stop feeding of a large crowd. That was probably why Anna looked more hassled than ever.

On election eve, all the supporters gathered in the compound. Municipal leaders, *Barangay* captains and village leaders from the various districts came to show their loyalty to the Rosales candidates, speaking in turns on a makeshift stage. When the speeches were done, a group of youth volunteers took over and started jamming with their guitars.

The next day, early in the morning, the Rosales clan drove to the voting precinct in full force. They were met by a group of poll watchers and volunteers at the entrance who ushered them to their precinct and voting booths. Claire and her relatives followed Ric's lead and cast their vote. A group of media people and cameramen waited for them at the exit and requested for an interview with Ric while the rest of the family looked on, smiling and waving at the crowd that had thickened by then. When the interview and photo operations were completed, the bodyguards ushered the family back to the waiting SUVs. While Ric tried to be jolly and cheerful at the precinct and during the interview, he became withdrawn once they were back in the war-room.

'We've done our best and I must say that from here on, God, as they say, will do the rest,' Mimi broke the prolonged silence.

'Ric, it's not the end of the world. I'm sure that you'll win this one like before. So stop being gloomy,' Cecille said, going over to sit on the arm of Ric's chair.

'I can't be too sure this time. Just now someone at the precinct whispered to me that Fernandez's camp distributed millions of pesos last night,' Ric shook his head.

'What? Shouldn't we report that to COMELEC?' Mimi interrupted, referring to the country's Commission on Elections, a government body tasked to enforce laws and regulations on elections.

'Yes, we can, and should, but we need to get credible witnesses,' Ric said. 'JM, can you call Noel and Leanne. I need to talk to them urgently.'

It was chaos from then on with Noel and Leanne running around mobilizing all their poll watchers and making sure none of the votes for Ric were stolen or nullified. Noel also started filing legal cases against Fernandez and contacting potential witnesses to back up the lawsuits.

The air in the war-room became even more stifling when the first reports came in towards midnight. 'Why is Fernandez leading now, I thought we had strong showing here,' Ric clenched his fist after pointing at the numbers.

'Daddy, that's his bailiwick,' JM replied.

'Why have they prioritized the counting there? Won't that set the tone? This would have negative psychological impact on our supporters,' Ric said.

'Sir, Fernandez's camp had urged their supporters to vote early. Besides the precincts in his district are smaller that's why they could finish the counting faster,' Noel explained.

Cecille urged Ric to go up and rest a bit as he only grew more restless with each new update, in turn making the team in the room more tensed.

'I'll be back in thirty minutes. JM, Mike, please man my phones and don't go anywhere else.' He reluctantly stepped out.

'Mimi, why don't you also go get some sleep,' Dino offered seeing that Mimi could not sit still.

'I can't,' Mimi replied.

'Then try to stretch out here,' Dino pointed at the reclining chair.

'I will in a while, but first let's check the San Fernando tally and see if any advantage there can help to reduce Fernandez's lead on the overall,' Mimi said.

In the end, none of the family members had gone off to sleep until the next day when Ric's numbers started catching up. It was the most tension-filled day for the family with many of the members crying at one point or another out of stress. Even JM and Mike who tried to be cool around Ric or Cecille had given in to the pressure and wept on Dino's shoulders when their parents had gone upstairs for a breather. Cecille's eyes were all red when she returned to the room. Ric could not settle down and decided to join his crew at the gazebo.

'Dino, the San Fernando votes are starting to trickle in,' Mimi asked Dino to check the numbers on the screen.

'Look, he's got forty thousand votes in already. JM call your Dad,' Dino said.

'How much of the vote have they counted now?' Cecille asked, going closer to the screen.

'It's more than sixty per cent. I think this trend should hold,' Mimi heaved a small sigh. She wiped away the tears that she could no longer stave off.

15

Singapore

'How was it?' Marc asked on the Monday Claire was back in office.

'Won by a tiny margin. For sure the other camp is going to protest as the margin is almost negligible,' Claire explained.

'Sounds like a big headache for your clan,' Marc added.

'Yep, but I guess they will manage. My aunt said all these twists and turns come with the territory. In any case, assuming the opponent motions for a recount, it will likely take the election commission years to resolve the case, and by then, it will be time for the next election cycle,' Claire shrugged her shoulders.

'Then it should not stop us from celebrating. So shall we go out tonight?' Marc asked.

'Yep, I need that badly. Should I round up the gang?' she said excitedly.

'Hmmm, I'm thinking just you and me,' Marc added, frowning slightly.

'Is something wrong?' Claire asked, seeing that Marc was unusually serious.

'There's something I really want to discuss with you, if that's all right,' Marc replied.

'Is everything okay with your family?' she asked.

'Yeah, they're good. I want to talk about something else. It just came up,' he replied as he stood up.

'Okay then. Sevenish?' she asked.

'Works for me. Later then,' he said before returning to his cubicle.

Claire could not remember ever seeing Marc in this mood in the past. There were times he got extremely frustrated with a client or two, but on those occasions, he was raring to fight back rather than having the beaten look he had now.

The rooftop bar at Ann Siang Hill was almost empty being a Monday and this could not have been any more conducive for the serious discussion that Marc had hinted at earlier. It overlooked a scenic portion of Chinatown, but this was largely lost on the two who were oblivious to their surroundings. Marc ordered a bellini for Claire and a manhattan for himself.

'What is it?' Claire could not wait to hear his story.

'Just a sec,' he said as he put his phone on silent mode.

'It's Steve actually,' he finally answered.

Claire gave a big sigh of relief. Based on the gravity of Marc's earlier expression, she had been scared that some sort of tragedy had struck Marc's family. Or worse, that he himself had found out he had a terminal disease. Claire, being Claire, had entertained all the worst-case scenarios. It never occurred to her that it would be something related to Steve.

'Why are you sounding so relieved?' Marc was surprised.

'You don't know how much I've dreaded this conversation. All afternoon I was worried that something awful had happened to your family. Or to you.'

'I don't know if this news is any easier though,' he replied. 'Steve wants me to join him in New York,' he said in a whisper.

Claire's frown suddenly cleared only to be replaced with a gasp. 'And are you?' she asked.

'I need to be with him, but I don't know how.'

'No, I don't want you to go,' Claire immediately reacted. 'But if you really want and need to, why don't you apply for cross-posting?' she added seeing that Marc was crestfallen.

'I already checked but there are no vacancies currently. Given the economic situation in the US now, no office would absorb me without a sound economic rationale.'

'When does he want you to be there?' she asked.

'ASAP, of course. The past few months without him in Singapore were also difficult for me. I'd gotten used to living with him,' he sighed. 'If only I could find a job in New York, it would solve half the problem,' he said, standing and walking around before sitting down again. He ordered a second round of drinks seeing that both their glasses were now empty.

'What's the other half of the problem?' Claire was puzzled.

'My family doesn't know about us yet. In the meantime, Steve is adamant about us getting married soon,' Marc sighed.

'How?' she asked.

'He said we could do it in Boston,' Marc said. 'There are talks that it will soon be legal in New York as well.'

'What to do? I wish I could do something, but this is very tricky.'

'I know. If only Mum and Dad were not so conservative and religious,' Marc sighed yet again for the umpteenth time.

'What about Josh? Do you think Josh would understand? Maybe you could break the news to him first and ask his help in handling the parents?'

'I've been thinking about that. In fact, I've already invited Josh for a short visit.'

'When is he coming?'

'Next month.'

'I'm sure things will turn out well eventually, but don't resign until you find a job in New York, or at least until Josh gives his approval. Not that you need the latter, but it will make things easier I suppose.'

'Look at you, you are talking as though from experience,' Marc sipped the last drop of his drink and motioned for the bill.

The ride home was uncomfortable as Marc was uncharacteristically silent. Claire tried to make small talk, but Marc simply put her head on his shoulder and wrapped his arms around her. Not that Claire was sleepy or anything, but she indulged him anyway.

While she sounded pragmatic earlier when advising Marc, Claire now found herself almost crying at the thought of Marc leaving. They would certainly remain connected on social media, though she knew that nothing could ever replace their regular face-to-face catch-ups and meaningful conversations. Marc was one of the most insightful individuals she knew, her favourite coffee buddy, and the only one she trusted with her personal travails. She would be unmoored without him. She remembered how Marc tried to cheer her up on that trip to Bangkok after her grandmother's death; how he always called when she was away on her family holidays; how he was there almost round-the-clock when she had an accident so much so that Anna had thought he was her boyfriend. Most importantly, she would always remember how he listened to her empathetically when she revealed who her true parents were. She had forgotten what life was like before Marc.

Both Claire and Marc remained gloomy the entire week as though they were mourning the death of a loved one. Some people in the office even noticed this lack of laughter or of teasing from either. They brought this gloominess with them to a new café near East Coast Park, where neither wanted any drink but a coffee even on a Friday night. He held her hand tightly as though it were a lifeline. Then he put his arm back around her shoulders. 'Now tell me,' he said.

'I'll be devastated when you go. You are my bestest friend, Marc. You know that. I don't really hang out with anyone else, apart from Pia and you. If it really were just up to me, I really wouldn't want you to go. I don't want to sound mushy, but I really wouldn't know what to do without you,' she said. She was never this expressive but grateful that this time around she could say what she genuinely felt.

'I wish Steve didn't have to go so that I don't have to follow,' Marc said. 'Wait, why can't you move to New York eventually? You have a family there, don't you?' he consciously lowered his voice on the last question.

'A family that I am yet to meet, except for Melanie.'

'Well . . . isn't it high time you met the rest?'

'I wish it were that easy, but things are more difficult to orchestrate with the great distance and the number of people involved. Anyway, there'll be a time for that. Right now is your time, let's focus on you first,' she said.

'I think it should go according to plan,' Marc smiled.

'I really hope so,' Claire hugged him spontaneously.

'Josh seems to have an inkling that I'm having an emotional crisis. He's coming sooner.'

'That's a positive sign. I hope he'll be supportive. He should be. He works in the entertainment industry,' she said.

'He's liberal, left-leaning as some people would say. He has several non-binary friends, too. Very gender sensitive. I hope he remains that way when it comes to his own brother,' Marc said in a serious tone.

'How can I help? Is there anything you want me to do when he is in town?'

'You can organize the dinners, and I'm thinking we should all go to Bintan on the weekend that he's here. What do you think?'

'Sure, we can go for a quick get-away, but why Bintan?'

'It's the easiest, that's why. We'll keep it simple. He is only here for a few days.'

'Okay, I'll book an overnight stay at Bintan then.'

16

Bintan, Indonesia

'Thanks for arranging this trip,' Josh said, going over to Claire's side on the view deck of the ferry en route to Club Med in Bintan.

'It's the least I could do. I'd do anything for Marc. He is the most important person for me in Singapore,' Claire said.

'I feel guilty that he had to hide his situation from us and I'm sad that he didn't trust me enough to share his issues sooner,' Josh added.

'Perhaps he was just being cautious given the distance and all. I suppose it's better to discuss things face-to-face, especially when high emotions are at stake. Having heard about how strict your parents are, I'd also have done the same if I were in his shoes,' she said.

'You both think so alike. No wonder you are friends,' Josh laughed.

'We've been working together for many years now so naturally we've picked up each other's quirks. The process is called osmosis,' she said.

'Yeah right. So this is the deadpan that Marc had been talking about.'

'What all did he say about me? Oh my God, I'm feeling embarrassed all of a sudden,' she covered her face with one hand.

'Oh, don't worry. Marc loves his friends to bits and he clearly adores you more than anyone else so he always talked about you in a positive light. Happy?' he asked, the corners of his eyes crinkling as he laughed.

'Haaa, now I can breathe,' she exaggerated.

They were soon at Club Med and by sunset Claire was walking with the brothers along the shore.

'Earlier I even thought you were his girlfriend. Perhaps that was why it never occurred to me that he'd be having these issues,' he said.

'Really? Did we give off that vibe?' she asked.

'I just assumed based on his earlier stories. But when I first met you at Prego you weren't doing PDAs in the physical sense. So I asked him right after we'd left the bar and that was when I learned you weren't a couple. I should have gotten an inkling after that, paid more attention, but obviously I had other things on my mind,' Josh looked at her intently.

'I would have proposed to him. He is such a fine specimen that it's a big loss for my tribe. But I'm glad that I really have a good friend in him,' Claire replied.

'Guys, keep it down, I can hear you,' Marc lunged at both of them. 'Now, if only Mum and Dad understood my situation, I'd be in total bliss. I have a feeling they'd be more concerned with what their fellow parishioners would say,' Marc said rubbing an eyebrow.

#

At the bar that evening, Claire untied her ponytail and literally let her hair down after her third glass of margarita. Marc, too, seemed to have lost all the tension that he had been carrying for weeks. 'That stroll around town was totally relaxing,' Marc said. 'Tonight . . . this night is ours. We're not going to worry about anything else,' he declared.

Soon after, Claire found herself up on the dancefloor with Marc and Josh. With Marc as their choreographer, they danced to all the iconic steps of the past decade. They also joined the band in singing the last song, Robyn's 'Dancing on my Own' that Marc had requested.

Claire was tipsy by the time they stepped off the stage and Josh quickly offered his hand while Marc was oblivious to any of these and kept on singing happily on the way out.

'I've been curious why your name doesn't start with M, unlike your siblings,' she asked while waiting for Marc, who was momentarily lost in the crowd. She knew from Marc that they had a sibling, Mia, who had died in a car accident.

'This is one little secret in the family. My first name also starts with M, but I dropped it after high school and decided to use just my middle name,' Josh answered.

'Really. What is it?'

'Haha, *it* is something you wouldn't get from me. Or from Marc,' Josh said.

'How sure are you that Marc won't divulge that info once you're out of earshot? Shall we find out?' she teased.

'Well, you can try. But don't blame me if you end up disappointed,' he replied. He seemed so very sure of Marc's loyalty that Claire could not help but admire this bond between the two.

'Let's see. What's at stake?' she bluffed.

'That's tempting. Let me think. What about you treating me to the most expensive dinner that you can afford? I heard there are several Michelin-starred restaurants in Singapore,' he laughed, seemingly confident about winning this one.

Marc emerged from behind another group and caught up with them and learned about the bet. 'Claire, margarita is clearly not your drink. You should stick to bellini next time,' Marc told her.

'The game isn't over yet. We shall continue tomorrow,' she said as they walked up the stairs to their rooms. 'I think I'm about to crash. Goodnight, guys, see you tomorrow,' she hugged both Marc and Josh before she went into her room.

'Are you okay?' Josh asked leaning on the doorframe.

Claire nodded.

'Claire, darling, let me help you to bed,' Marc offered.

'Thanks Marc, but I'm fine. You're not in any better state, my dear,' Claire said, seeing that Marc was more drunk than usual.

'We're in the next room if you need help,' Josh, the only sober one of the three, offered.

'Thanks, Josh. But I think I can manage. Goodnight,' she said before closing the door.

#

The next day, Claire tried to extract information about Josh's real name but Marc would not cooperate. 'No way can you get that info from me, Miss Rosales,' he said.

'Please, please, Louise,' she begged childishly.

'No emotional manipulations. I owe you big time, we both know that, but don't be unfair,' Marc was amused at the way she begged.

'Fine. There goes my three hundred bucks then if your brother is serious about claiming the prize.'

'Josh will. Don't worry. He hardly ever says things he won't do,' Marc patted her hand in consolation.

'Okay, lesson learned. This will definitely be charged to experience.'

'And to your Visa or MasterCard,' Marc almost spilled his coffee as he laughed at his own joke.

'On to other more important topics. Are you happy about how things are turning out for you?' she asked.

'Definitely. I really love Josh. I can't do this without his support. It's true what they say about how some crises can bring out the best, or the worst, in people. Josh has always been a good brother, but I didn't really expect him to be this supportive. I saw his best side on this visit,' Marc said.

'I'm so happy for you. Now I suppose half the battle is won,' Claire smiled.

'Yep, you could say that. It's still an uphill climb from here, but with Josh's support, I now have the guts to try,' Marc said.

'I'm sure it's not as grim as you think. I should remember that you, too, are a worst-case scenario type of person,' she added.

'True that. But then, that's how I survive. It's difficult being me as I'm sure you know,' he smiled before waving at Josh, who was on his way to join them for breakfast.

With Josh around, breakfast became livelier as they recounted last night's escapades and the brothers resumed teasing Claire about her impending loss.

'Remind me not to make any bets with Josh next time. My knowledge of Game Theory is totally useless here,' she told Marc. She shifted her gaze to Josh, 'But why did you tempt me. I thought you're the kind one,' she said.

'Whoa, wait. Who said anything about kindness?' Josh said.

'Who else do you think?' she replied.

'Oh man, I really love you, Marc. I wonder how many more of your friends think I'm an angel,' Josh winked at Marc.

'Come on, Josh, please tell Claire what your official name is. Don't be shy. She won't tell another soul about it,' Marc said.

'Shut up, Marc. Next topic, please,' he prompted.

'Like the script that you're writing for Paramount?' Marc added.

'You are writing for a giant studio?' Claire knew that Josh was a scriptwriter, but she did not know that he worked with big studios. He never mentioned this in their earlier discussions.

'Marc,' Josh tried to shush him.

'Yes, Marc,' Marc teased. 'We must remember that Josh never trumpets his triumph. Ouch that's a painful alliteration,' he said, grinning mischievously.

'I'm not supposed to talk about it, not at this stage anyway. But yes, I'm writing a script for a small division of Paramount. And that's all I can say about the matter,' Josh said as he waved at the waiter to place his order.

#

Singapore

Claire's life in Singapore, while orderly and peaceful, was uneventful. Apart from Marc and Pia, she only had a few friends in the city-state as most of her long-time friends had moved to the United States, Canada, or other parts of the world. Her social life had become duller when Marc had started going out with Steve although Marc had done his best to include her in their outings whenever possible. Claire had gone with the two on some of the couple's weekend trips, but she had tried to avoid being a 'third-wheeler'. The trip to Bintan with Marc and Josh was the most fun she had in a long time.

When the time came for Josh to collect on the bet, he did not insist on an expensive dinner but asked for a coffee instead. Claire took him to an artisanal coffee shop housed in a nondescript building that looked almost like a hardware store in Little India. Claire felt justified in her choice when she found out that Josh was serious about his coffee, the type who would wrinkle his nose at ubiquitous global coffee chains that offered countless permutations of diluted coffee. He selected a single estate brew from Java while she tried one from Ethiopia.

'Marc was right to be worried knowing Mum and Dad and the way they react to news of same-sex marriages. Frankly, if I were in Marc's shoes, I wouldn't have the guts to tell them about it, but Marc is their favourite. He was always an achiever in school and that made them truly proud of him earlier on. And after what happened to Mia, I'm sure they would not want to lose another child,' Josh said, as he placed the tray on the table and handing Claire her coffee.

'What do you mean?'

'Marc is utterly serious about Steve and I know he could stand being disowned by the parents if it came to that. That's the worst-case scenario, though—I doubt if Mum and Dad would want to go through that. I'm thinking out loud here. Sorry,' he said before taking a sip of his coffee. 'Anyway, let's talk about something else. Something more fun,' he smiled.

'What is fun for you? And by that I suppose politics is off?' Claire asked.

He laughed and said, 'Yes, politics is definitely off. While I'm open to other perspectives and beliefs, I'm passionate about my own and I tend to argue a lot about political issues. I don't think you'd find that fun. So, let's not go there.'

'I don't like politics either. And politicians. Let's talk about movies then, as I'm sure you're an expert on the subject. What's your all-time favourite? And why is it your favourite?' she asked.

'Is it your turn to interview me now? That sounds like an essay question. Or a beauty-pageant question,' he said almost snorting.

'I'm in the business of asking questions, remember?'

'Okay, why don't you make a guess? If you get it correctly then I will answer the "why" part objectively.'

'*The Godfather*?' she knew this to be a favourite of her cousins and other guy friends.

'Which one?'

'Part II?'

'Nope. Wrong answer. I'm sorry, you've just lost a one-in-a-million chance to hear my "insights" about my favourite movie and what makes it my favourite,' he smiled and motioned for the bill. They fought over the bill, but in the end, Claire managed to persuade him that it was her treat having lost in their earlier bet.

17

Singapore

'No tears, you promised me. We'll FaceTime every day and we'll see each other again in three months anyways. Besides, I'll still be visiting every now and then in my new role,' Marc said after checking-in for his flight to New York.

Only last night, Claire had organized a send-off party for Marc at the newly opened Marina Bay Sands rooftop bar. After the party, the group sat near the infinity pool and practically waited for daybreak by the loungers before eventually crawling to the suite Claire had reserved for the team. Claire then dashed off with Marc to the airport.

Reality finally struck Claire when they reached the immigration gate. She felt an acute loss and anchorless more than ever. 'It won't be the same,' Claire said. A lump was growing in her throat. Marc was her closest friend ever. She had never bared her inner self to anyone else. That was her nature. Except with Marc, who did not judge her at all, and accepted her and loved her for what she was. 'I know it will hit me hardest on Monday, when I reach office and you won't be there any more. Who will I have coffee with? Who will I have lunch with?' she asked. This was the first thing that came to her mind and the easiest to articulate, but she knew that Marc was much more than just her coffee or lunch buddy. He filled many cracks in her life. He made her feel whole when she felt broken.

'Then you know what to do. I will look out for opportunities for you. Hopefully we can all be together in New York soon,' Marc hugged her once more and kissed her on the forehead before entering the immigration gate.

Claire did not know what to do with the rest of her day. It did not help that it was a Saturday. She avoided heading straight home, as she might get more depressed. She stopped by Starbucks at the terminal and found a table by the window that looked out to the sky and the planes that were departing, leaving behind only their contrails, and fleetingly at that. She watched as one zoomed past, forming a diagonal contrail. She had been in many flights that left Singapore for various destinations. She knew what it felt to be on board a departing plane. Sometimes there was excitement. Sometimes there was dread. But this was the first time she was left behind. Soon the contrails were gone, merging with the feathery clouds of the day. And yet she could not shake off this feeling of aloneness. She was alone in this vibrant city. There was not much to look forward to in the coming days.

18

Singapore

On one of their get-togethers, Claire met Pia in the weekend market at Red Dot Museum. Pia did her best to cheer Claire up, to the point of mimicking the funny faces on the post cards they picked up from one of the stalls. From there, they went to River Valley for late lunch, then walked down to Robertson Quay, checking out the small boutiques in the area and even stopping by at the Singapore Tyler Print Institute. When the air was cooler, they walked yet again along the Singapore River, stopping at the colourful Alkoff Bridge—sometimes referred to as the Pacita Abad Art Bridge—where Pia tried funny postures and forced Claire to take 'more flattering' photos of each pose.

'If this wonderful burst of colours can't cheer you up, then nothing else can,' Pia said, after striking yet another pose.

'I already feel a bit better, thanks as always. Coming here is really a great idea. This is the first time I'm crossing this bridge, can you imagine?' she said.

'Congratulations. So, you've just *literally* crossed a bridge,' Pia laughed even harder.

'Yep, after hearing about it from so many people,' she said.

In the evening both were too tired to go anywhere else and decided to head back to Claire's apartment for a girls' night-in.

Claire ordered their favourite four-cheese pizza from Pepperoni and Pia appointed herself the Chief Decision Maker for their movie that night.

#

Pia kept inviting Claire to one event after another and that helped fill Claire's time, now that Marc was away. On yet another weekend, Claire tried to sleep in a bit more before meeting Pia for brunch but was awakened by an early morning call from Mimi.

'Hello, Auntie, what is it?' Claire asked, shaking off the last traces of sleep, and surprised to get a call from Mimi this early.

'Claire, I just got a call from Cecille.'

'And?'

'Ric has just told her about you.'

'Without any of us there? Why couldn't he wait for us to be there so that we could control any damage?' she said.

'Apparently they were having a big fight. About something else. And Ric simply dropped the latest about you. Along with other things that Cecille has been clueless about,' Mimi rattled on.

'What's wrong with him?'

'I'm on the verge of losing it as far as Ric is concerned. But I'm also worried about Dino. I don't want him to be facing all these issues by himself. I'm going for a quick visit and I'm begging you to join me. Your daddy needs us.'

'Please tell everyone to calm down. This is a thirty-year-old story. Why is everyone reacting only now? If anyone had the right to have an outsized reaction it should have been me. And I had restrained myself to help Uncle Ric win that damn election.'

'Look, I can never thank you enough for your restraint. But things are not the same any more since Mama's death, as you, yourself keep saying.'

#

Santa Rosa, Valle Viejo

Once again, Claire and Mimi found themselves on their way home to Santa Rosa, this time under the guise of attending Valle Viejo's 150th founding anniversary upon the invitation of the governor. There was no fanfare along the approach to the Rosales mansion except for the buntings and the big banner of greeting by the gate. The main celebrations were taking place in the capital city of San Fernando and less so in towns like Santa Rosa.

It was unusually quiet in the Rosales house such that even the slightest sound from the kitchen at the back of the house could be heard all the way in the drawing room. The characteristic chatter of the house staff was missing. Maritess almost wept upon seeing Mimi and Claire. She seemed like she wanted to say something but kept biting her lips.

That afternoon at the Rosales house, the clan members were once again huddled in the library, but this time for something far more serious than the last election. The only difference now was Ric's notable absence. He had stormed out of the house earlier when Mimi had suggested they discuss the situation in a more civil manner.

'We are going our separate ways,' Cecille said.

'Because of me?' Claire almost spluttered the coffee she had just sipped.

'No, it's not just that,' Cecille started crying and could not talk properly.

'Daddy has been having an affair,' JM filled in.

'With whom?' Claire asked.

'With a younger aide,' Mike replied.

She was about to blurt out something when she saw Dino signal to her that Mimi wanted to say something.

'But Cecille, what did he say? Isn't he ending his relationship with this other woman?' Mimi asked.

'No, he didn't say anything. Even if he were, I cannot take any more of his philandering, this one and all the earlier ones. It's just too much,' Cecille said, wiping off fresh tears. 'JM and Mike understand how I feel, and they fully support my decision. I am leaving this house and will be staying at our place in La Vista from now on. I've already told Ric to vacate the place.'

'Cecille, isn't this too drastic?' Mimi tried again.

'Not if you're living with a farce like Ric every day,' Cecille said.

Mimi flinched but kept quiet. Claire did not say anything but could relate to how Cecille felt. Dino was breathing deeply beside her.

'I'm sorry, Mimi, Dino. I'm not going to do anything scandalous. Not because of Ric. But because of Mike,' Cecille added, looking at Mike who was standing beside her.

'Thank you, Mummy,' Mike hugged Cecille. 'I don't need to hang on to my post, if that's what you mean,' he added.

'No, Mike, you must carry on. It's bad enough that I'm leaving my post. Your dad has failed, but you will not,' Cecille added forcefully. 'I'm going back to Quezon City with JM tomorrow. I'm sorry Mimi, Dino, but I can't stay here any longer given the situation,' Cecille said.

'Cecille, I don't know what to say. If it were just up to me, I would like you to stay and sort this out with Ric when he comes back. But I also can't force things if your decision is final. As you've just said, you're the one who has to deal with this situation every day,' Mimi said.

'He's not likely to come back while I'm here so I'd better go soon so that you could at least talk to him during this visit,' Cecille said.

#

'When did you learn about me?' Claire asked JM and Mike after the older relatives had left the room.

'Mummy told us earlier this week. It doesn't change anything between us. If at all, this makes our bond even stronger as I've always looked on you as my real sister anyway,' JM said.

'Same here, *Ate*,' Mike nodded, coming over to hug Claire.

'It's unfortunate that some people got hurt in the process,' Claire said, patting Mike's shoulder. 'I'm so worried about Tita Cecille,' Claire said.

'I don't know enough to say that Mummy's decision is the right one. But it's Mummy's life and I respect her decision,' JM said. 'Apparently there were others in the past, but obviously we're always the last to know,' JM stood and walked to the large window.

'Where does that leave us?' Mike also followed JM.

JM turned around to face Mike, 'I love Daddy, but right now I'm terribly disappointed with him for doing this to Mummy and for risking our reputation. He should have stopped after he got caught the first time,' he said, pressing his hands to his forehead.

'I know, *Kuya*. Right now, I don't want to talk to Daddy. How could he do this to us? I still can't believe that Mummy is leaving this house,' Mike continued to shake his head.

Claire thought they had been through the darkest days of the Rosales mansion when her grandmother passed away. At least then, they, the bereaved clan, had been united and Claire had found some degree of comfort in that. She had seen the best of the clan as they tried to overcome their sorrow together. Now that unity was collapsing due to Ric and Cecille's separation.

Ric was not a cement that could keep the clan together. Instead, he was an agent of disintegration. He was corrosive like acid that destroyed everything it touched. Mimi lived too far for everyday intervention while Dino preferred to be low-key and was busy with the farms. Rebuilding the clan's reputation now rested on Claire's generation. JM and Claire had requested Mike to take care of the Rosales House for now. Initially Mike hesitated given his duties as mayor of Santa Rosa, but with JM's and Claire's promises to support him wherever required he eventually accepted.

'So how do we inform Uncle Ric about Mike's moving back here?' Claire asked.

'Daddy is hardly here in Santa Rosa. I doubt if he'd even notice,' JM replied.

'But given his current disposition, wouldn't he insist that we need his 'permission'?' Claire said.

'His permission is no longer required because he has broken his contract with us,' Mike declared.

'He doesn't have any choice on this one,' JM added.

'Do you know where he is right now?' she asked.

'He's probably at Mayor Cruz's rest house in San Agustin,' Mike replied.

'This is such a nightmare,' Claire felt drained now.

'This must be what "adulting" means. We are forced to deal with problems we did not create,' JM sighed.

'*Ate, Kuya*, please. We are all capable. We can get through this together. We might be bruised right now, but we're not going to give up that easily,' Mike was the only one who sounded positive.

'Ah, that's why you have been rightfully elected as mayor,' JM came over to massage Mike's shoulder.

'You really are a true leader.' Claire also gave him a salute. 'Thanks for your wisdom today, Mike,' she started to smile. All three even reverted to their childhood gesture of putting their hands together as a promise to stick to each other come what may.

#

That night in her room, Claire kept tossing and turning on her bed but could not fall asleep however hard she tried. Fresh air might have helped but she did not want to step out of the room as it might disturb Dino or Anna who were both light sleepers. Ultimately she decided to simply curl up under her blanket and confront the thoughts that tormented her all evening. While she had kept her emotions under control when she was with her relatives, Claire had been fuming underneath; her disgust with Ric had grown ever more upon learning about his recent extramarital fiasco. She was unknowingly hitting her pillow in anger. How could Ric be so selfish and immoral? Did he not realize that his actions could easily lead to a huge scandal and destroy their family name forever? Did he not care about the Rosales clan at all that he, himself, would break it apart? Claire remembered one of her earlier interactions with Ric in the war-room and how he had challenged her data interpretation. Claire knew his tactic. He tried to intimidate lesser mortals by throwing his weight around, by staring them down or instilling doubt in themselves. What a big farce. She also remembered that she could stand up to him, she was not afraid of him. Congressman Big Farce did not have the right to ruin the Rosales family name. It was her and JM's and Mike's family name. She needed to tell Ric exactly that.

The next day Claire went to the Rosales House early in the morning hoping to find Ric there, knowing that he usually got up before anyone else. She found him in the dining room having coffee by himself.

'I've been wanting to talk to you,' she said, not bothering to sit.

'What about?' he didn't try to sound polite, but was visibly startled to see her. He pushed the newspaper to the side and looked at her.

'Everything.'

'Everything? Isn't that so vague?'

'I know everything,' she said, 'and I can never forgive you for what you've done. I've not said anything in the past out of respect for Daddy and Auntie Mimi. But the time is up. I'm more than ready to go to public and tell them exactly who you are.'

'What are you talking about?' he said, putting his coffee mug down.

'I don't want you to do any more damage to the family. Especially to JM, Mike and me. We also carry the Rosales name and we have more moral right than you to this family name. I want you to leave this house, leave Santa Rosa. Never run for any political position again in Valle Viejo,' she warned him.

'Who are you to stop me?' he said, standing up now.

'You'll find out soon enough if you don't do the things I've just said. You've done enough damage in this lifetime. You should be ashamed of yourself. You're worse than a scumbag,' she said and was about to leave when Ric grabbed her shoulder and spun her around to face him.

'Do you think the public have no clue? Do you think whatever revelation you have will change their minds? That's the problem with people like you. You're too wrapped up in your own dainty world. Spending a few days in a year here does not give you the right to talk to me like an expert. You clearly don't have any inkling on what makes these local people tick. Unfortunately, or fortunately, not everyone is on a high horse like you.'

'It doesn't matter. I'm still going to call a press conference and tell them what you truly are,' she said, making another attempt to leave.

'Sit down. Let me tell you who I really am. I am the one who has been forced by this clan into many things that are not my choice, starting with my own marriage. I've been the one forced to wear this public face while all of you enjoy your so-called privacy. Do you realize how difficult it is to keep on smiling even when these goddamn peasants think they can fool me? No, of course you don't have a clue, because in your frivolous little world, you don't need to shake hands with real peasants.'

'Stop it. You're merely trying to justify your evil acts,' Claire said.

'You started this, Claire, so you might as well get a clearer idea of what my glamorous job entails. Who do you think takes the blame when someone else from the clan makes a mess of things? You were probably too young to have heard about your grandfather, but who do you think took the blame for some public projects he mismanaged? I was the convenient scapegoat, Claire. And when he supported a governor who subsequently lost the election, what do you think was his best solution? You can make a guess. Yes, forcing me to marry Cecille even when we were not ready, just so he could align himself with the winning party.'

'That's not what I've heard.'

'What do you know when you are wrapped so comfortably in your fluffy cocoon. Besides, nobody would want to pollute your clean little ears with this kind of murky stuff.'

'Even if these were all true, you could have made a better choice and made things right instead of resuming with your series of affairs. You were given a chance to clean up your mess and yet you chose to keep on misleading women.'

'Who says anything about misleading? In all these affairs, it's the women who came to me, not the other way around.'

'That excuse is overused. You were in the position of power. You took advantage of the women's situations.'

'Easy for you to say, Saint Claire, when you're not in the middle of any of these situations,' he said, before leaving the room in a huff.

Claire rushed out to the waiting car and told the driver to take her back home. It took a while before the shaking stopped, but she did not mention the confrontation to anyone else. Later that day, she heard from Mike that Ric had already left for Manila for some congressional session or another, in one of his foulest moods.

19

Singapore

'Oh my God, what did they say?' Claire could not help but jump in her excitement while listening to Marc on the phone. Marc had visited his parents in California and finally found the courage to tell them about himself and Steve.

'You should have seen their facial expressions. They were utterly shocked. Despite Josh's support, they didn't talk to me for an entire day,' Marc said.

'Dear Lord, it must have been very awkward and painful for you,' she said.

'It was. But because of Josh, oh I owe Josh my life, they spoke to me again at breakfast the next day,' Marc added.

'So, all is well that ends well then,' she said.

'Not exactly. They still won't come to the wedding, but said that I can go ahead with it,' Marc replied.

'That's sad,' Claire sighed.

'But Josh said this is Mum and Dad's version of tacit acceptance. So I should just count my blessings,' he said.

#

New York

The rooftop of Marc's apartment building was transformed into a cosy garden with flowers and colourful fairy lights for their wedding reception in New York. A caterer and a barista served canapés and drinks, which Josh pretended to keep swiping before distributing the 'goods' to the guests around him. Soon, it was Josh's turn to give a toast that he did so eloquently that it was received with much applause from the guests. He came to sit beside Claire afterwards. 'Congrats, that was an awesome toast,' she shook his hand.

'Thanks. I actually prepared a more formal speech but, in the end, I decided to throw it away and just do it off-the-cuff,' he said picking one of the canapés from the passing waiter.

'You were so articulate it's easy to assume you'd rehearsed that speech at least a million times. But then again, there was nothing wooden about the delivery, an indication of how genuine your emotions were,' she noted.

'Thanks for the insightful analysis. I guess that's what happens when one speaks from the heart, as they say,' he nodded.

Later that night, a DJ arrived and started playing music. At first, Claire and Josh were happy just listening to the songs, but when other guests started heading to the dance floor, Josh took Claire's hand and before she knew it, they were lost in the crowd dancing to the Black Eyed Peas and other upbeat songs of the 2000s. In between, when Claire was out of breath, Josh pulled her into his arms and they danced to slower tunes. At midnight, the guests broke into shouts when boxes of Chinese takeaway were delivered. More champagne bottles were brought out and louder cheers immediately followed each pop. It was almost dawn when the wedding party sent off Marc and Steve into the elevator down to their apartment in preparation for their trip to Costa Rica.

The next day, Claire had brunch with Josh at a café near her hotel. 'Thanks for getting up so early after that very late night,' Claire greeted.

'Oh please. Let's not be so polite here. By the way, I'm relatively free without any agenda for the day so I'm quite happy to take you around this big city,' Josh said.

'I don't want to take up so much of your time. Besides I know my way around here,' Claire hesitated.

'It will be ten times more fun if you go with a certified guide, like me. I can give you some insider tips and insights as well. Don't you love insights? I used to live here for six years, so I know some of the places you've only read about,' Josh said in his salesman voice.

'If you have the time, then, yes, I'm more than happy to follow you around now that Rinka has left for New Jersey,' she accepted his offer.

'Great. I'm even throwing in a couple of Broadway plays into the offer. What say you?' he asked.

'That's so generous of you. Who, in her right mind, would refuse a Broadway offer?' she smiled.

'Glad you have your head on your shoulders then. I'll swing by after your meet-up with Melanie,' Josh added as soon as they reached her hotel lobby for the second time in only the last twelve hours.

'Yep, see you then,' Claire waved at him as he headed out.

#

In the evening, she walked down to a French café near the Grand Central Station. Melanie was already there, reading a book by the glass window. She quickly got up to hug Claire upon her entrance. 'It's been a while,' Melanie said, gesturing to the chair across from hers.

'Time flies as they say. It's hard to believe but it's been more than a year,' Claire noted.

'Thanks to your friend's wedding, I get to see you again after a lo . . . oo . . . ong time,' Melanie said.

Claire ordered her flat white as usual. She also tried the salted caramel crepe that Melanie suggested. They talked about culinary trends triggered by Claire's interest of the salted caramel craze.

'Do you know what Nate and Melissa's favourite dish is? Take a guess,' Melanie asked.

'Steak?' Claire said.

'Ah would you believe that they love, loo . . . oove my own version of chicken and pork adobo or the so-called CPA back in Manila. It's become their comfort, and all-occasion, dish,' Melanie said proudly.

'Wow,' Claire was amused, recalling her chicken adobo phase back in her grade school convent.

Melanie loved to cook, as cooking helped her decompress. 'I totally adore Ina Garten and Julia Child,' she said.

'That's interesting. I too have Julia Child's recipe book,' Claire said.

'What made you buy Julia Child?' Melanie asked.

'I watched *Julie and Julia* on one of my flights,' Claire replied.

'I was so impressed with Meryl Streep in that movie. Well, I've always liked Meryl Streep, but even more so in that film,' Melanie said.

After their plates were cleared and only the coffee cups remained on their table, Melanie mentioned the upcoming meeting. 'Nate and Melissa are in town and they are excited to meet you finally. I'm hoping you're available this Saturday so we could have brunch together,' Melanie smiled.

'Saturday works for me. It would really be good if we could meet this time. I'm flying out on Sunday,' she replied.

'Wonderful. I'll confirm the venue later,' Melanie said, immediately inputting the date to her mobile calendar. 'Oh, Claire, I'm trying to be brave about all this, but you must know I'm a bundle of nerves and mixed emotions inside. I've given it a lot of thought and I know that the time has come for you to meet each other.'

'I believe the same. There's a time and season for everything. We're all grown up now and I'm sure we'll manage somehow,' Claire said, trying to be positive as well.

'Thanks for being so understanding. Anyway, what are your plans between now and Saturday?' Melanie asked.

'I'm watching a couple of Broadway shows with a friend and I'm also checking out some of the bookshops,' she replied.

'Sounds exciting. I'm sure you'll have fun at the bookstores. There's so many of them that you'll never run out of options. I'm glad you have friends here who can take you around,' she said.

'Yep, some of them are from the wedding party. Josh, one of them, is Marc's older brother. He's coming to pick me up later, so you'll get to meet him,' Claire added.

'Great. That reduces my guilt for not having taken days off to show you around,' Melanie exhaled in exaggeration to show her relief. 'By the way, how is Marc? I've only met him once when I was in Singapore, but I remember him being very nice. He has a very positive aura,' she added.

'I've never seen him happier,' Claire replied. She was oblivious to the time until she saw Josh walking towards them from across the street.

Melanie invited Josh to join them, which he graciously accepted. Within five minutes Melanie was laughing at one of his anecdotes about his years in the city. At the end of their chat, Claire offered to split the bill, but Melanie insisted it was on her.

'I get easily irritated by these all-knowing cabbies that I end up either walking or taking the subway whenever I can,' Melanie said, when they were about to leave. 'Even after all these years here, I've never really gotten used to the smell of the cabs,' she wrinkled her nose.

Josh instantly looked at Claire with that eureka expression because Claire wrinkled her nose in exactly the same manner.

#

A visit to New York was not complete without watching a Broadway play, and Claire had Josh to thank for making this trip complete. They watched *Wicked*. To be fair, it was Claire's choice. She joined the audience in the never-ending applause at curtain call. Josh claimed to have enjoyed it as well, but admitted he would not have watched it on his own. He then took her to a cosy café off Broadway where they spent almost two hours comparing notes on the plays they had watched in the past. In his six years in New York, Josh had practically watched all the Tony Awards winners of the past decade. On the other hand, Claire had watched only a few plays at Broadway.

Josh dropped Claire off at her hotel and promised to be at her doorstep by ten the next day for the much-anticipated bookstore hopping, perhaps the best way to prepare for a potentially stressful situation. Although Melanie had assured her that Nate and Melissa were polite and generally well brought-up, this did not reduce Claire's anxiety about meeting them. Josh noticed this. 'Look, I know this is a very unusual situation, but don't let it stress you so much,' he said.

'I guess I'm scared of being judged, but, come to think of it, they must be feeling the same too,' Claire said.

'Precisely. The burden shouldn't be on you alone. Anyway, just be chill about it. I'll be near your meeting place tomorrow and I'll pick you up within five minutes of your call in the worst of scenarios.'

'I'm sure it won't come to that. They have no reason to be rude.'

'Of course. Having met Melanie, she does not seem to be the type who would tolerate ill-mannered children,' Josh said, holding her hand as they crossed the street to her hotel.

'Do you want to come up for coffee? There's a café on the fourth floor,' she offered, once they reached the lobby.

'Only if you really want to. But I'd rather you went to bed early so you'll be fresh and alert tomorrow,' he suggested.

'Ah well, you're right. Besides, I think we've had enough coffee for the day, was it three cafés today?' she asked as she took her books from him.

'I've stopped counting,' he laughed. 'I'll see you after your brunch then,' he said pulling her towards him and kissing her on the forehead.

'Thanks again,' she said, hugging him tighter this time and as she did so, he could feel Josh rubbing her shoulder blade gently. 'I could get used to this,' she teased.

'I'm only too happy to provide this kind of service, mademoiselle. But please choose a better location next time, a less crowded one perhaps,' Josh said, as he straightened up and pointed at the waiting elevator. He waited until she was in the elevator before he stepped out into the streets of Manhattan.

That night, Claire switched off all the lights in her room and opened her curtains to look at the Manhattan skyline. As she stared at the towers and the neon lights, she could not help but notice the vast difference between this city and her hometown. Here, the reflections brightened the room even when the lights inside were switched off. In Santa Rosa, on the other hand, it could be pitch-black at eight o'clock in the evening, especially in the rainy season. The townsfolk generally turned in early. If ever lights were left on, they tended to be the low-wattage and dim variety. In a way, this was a blessing, as the children could still see the fireflies that swarmed around trees after the rain. As a kid, Claire used to watch from her window when fireflies would cluster around the bougainvillea near the gate of their house.

Claire also recalled that the quietness at Santa Rosa could be deafening at times, especially when the TV and radio were turned off. Even at the Rosales House, most of the staff usually wrapped up their chores and returned to their respective families before dinner. All the attendant noise such as the clanging and banging of kitchen utensils as well as the staff's friendly bickering went with them. The staff that stayed in, including Maritess, were soft-spoken. Claire remembered being spooked out by the stillness that felt like midnight even when it was only eight o'clock in the evening.

The sound of zooming cars and the blasting of horns brought Claire back to her New York present. It was not unusual to hear sirens from an ambulance or a police car every so often. While she loved the arts-and-culture scene in New York, the noise was something that bothered her. She mentally berated herself for even thinking this and reminded herself not to say anything about this in front of her half-siblings tomorrow.

Early the next day, Claire chose a strong coffee pod, carried her mug to bed, and sat cross-legged as she sipped her coffee. Her anxiety had returned, perhaps triggered by the caffeine she had just ingested, but could have also been because of the long overdue meeting that was only a few hours away. She checked her phone and saw a message from Josh, reminding her that he would be five-minutes away any time she needed him that morning. Marc also sent a message full of heart and hug emoticons. Apart from the two, she had not told anyone else about the meeting with Melanie and her family. In hindsight, she was glad she did this, because she could not deal with any fuss from family and friends. She wondered what her family's reaction would have been had they known that today was not just another ordinary Saturday in her life.

At nine-thirty in the morning, she hailed a cab that took her to a rustic place called Brunch and Beyond beside a boutique hotel in Lower Manhattan. She entered the restaurant and scanned the place. She saw Melanie reading the menu at a round table in the corner. Frank was sitting beside her and it was he who noticed Claire's arrival first. He tapped Melanie's arm before getting up to fetch Claire.

'Claire, good to see you again,' Frank hugged her before ushering her to their table.

Melanie jumped up from her chair and hugged Claire as though she had not seen her for years even though they had met each other only the other day.

'Hi,' Claire greeted Nate and Melissa who were also standing now. Claire was not usually the first to greet a new acquaintance, but thinking she was older than the two, she exerted greater effort and tried to look more enthusiastic.

'I've heard so much about you and couldn't wait to meet you,' Nate hugged her warmly. He was tall and lanky and wearing wire-rimmed glasses. He took after Frank's complexion and was fairer than Melanie.

'Hi, welcome to New York,' said Melissa, hugging Claire briefly. Melissa was as tall as Melanie and took after her in more ways than one.

When everyone was seated, Melanie passed the menu to Claire, who in turn stared at it for a while as she tried to get her bearings. 'Everything looks good, what would you recommend?' she eventually asked the siblings.

'I love the rosti with eggs benedict and mozzarella,' Nate beamed.

'He orders exactly the same thing whenever we come here,' Melissa said. 'I don't know what that says about him, though,' she added, raising two fingers and making the peace sign to Nate.

'Now I'm very curious about this dish. I'll order the same,' Claire smiled at how Nate and Melissa were still teasing each other in sign language.

'These two never grew up. They're no different from when they were pre-schoolers,' Melanie said, her eyes gleaming with pride.

While waiting for their food, Frank steered the conversation to the current Broadway shows. This helped Claire relax a little. 'I've just watched *Wicked* the other day and it was amazing,' she shared.

'I love it, too. And I don't mind watching it again. And again. I love the musical scoring and I've been singing 'For Good' even in my sleep I think,' Melissa laughed.

'She sings it very well . . . in the bathroom,' Nate said.

Melissa turned her peace sign down at Nate. She looked at Claire. 'You know what else you should watch? *Mamma Mia*. Mum loves it to bits,' she smiled.

'And Dad just dozed off as usual,' Nate added with a poker face.

Later on, Melissa asked about Claire's work and grew curious when Claire started talking about her knowledge of the various skincare habits and practices in the Asia Pacific region. Meanwhile, Nate beamed every time they talked about literature, which was in line with his liberal-arts course. Claire could not help but note some similarities between him and Frank in academic leanings and physical features. Nate, however, was more expressive than Frank. He was more a version of Melanie in this area, in a dignified manner that did not call attention to himself.

Everyone seemed nice and the food was great, but Claire was relieved when brunch was over. It was difficult to connect one-on-one in this setting, though she was glad that she had hurdled the initial challenge of meeting the siblings for the first time.

'I'll drop you off at the airport tomorrow; what time do you need to be there?' Nate asked.

'Thanks, Nate. But my friend has promised to do that. Perhaps you could have the honour on my next trip?' she ventured.

Nate was disappointed, but asked Claire to reserve this 'honour' for him next time. Melissa also promised to take her out shopping during her next visit.

#

Claire came out of the restaurant feeling lighter than when she went in. She was smiling to herself as she looked for Josh, who was waiting for her at the next block. She could see that he read her expressions well, because he beamed at her immediately.

'See, I told you, there was nothing to fear but fear itself,' he said as he hugged her.

'I know. I was anxious for nothing. I should have more faith in humanity,' she closed her eyes in relief.

'I thought your faith had already been restored the first time you saw me,' Josh said with a poker face.

'Yeah, right. And speaking of another person who thinks highly of himself, it's your brother.' She replied to the call and gave Marc the headlines from this morning.

Josh draped his hand over her shoulders as they walked towards yet another bookshop. He promised this was different, being an independent shop specializing in rare and vintage copies. It was huge and it overwhelmed Claire so much that she could not decide what to buy. In the end, she bought only one item, a vintage copy of *An Old Man and the Sea*, which she planned to give Dino for Christmas.

That night, Josh invited her to dinner at Union Square Café. Everything was well and good but after tasting a few cocktail varieties, Claire started feeling tipsy. 'Oh my goodness, I don't think this complicated stuff is my kind of drink. Not this kind for sure. It has too much alcohol content,' Claire said.

'Are you feeling dizzy?' Josh looked concerned.

'No, not really, but I feel lightheaded,' she started giggling uncharacteristically. 'Don't worry, I should be fine after a glass of water,' she assured him. Then suddenly she started feeling sad. 'Oh gosh, I don't know what's happening. I feel like I should tell you more about myself, but then again, I shouldn't,' she said.

'Oh, come on. You can tell me anything. I'm not the judging type. I know you think of me as perfect, but I have my warts, too, you know what I mean,' he smiled.

'Seriously. Now I'm going to tell you yet another secret, and after this, tell me if you still think I'm someone you'd like to be with,' she said, smiling sadly.

'Oh my Lord, Claire. I can't take it when you look sad,' he said, putting his glass down and leaning over to hug her.

'I just want to bare the real me once and for all. You can take me or leave me after this,' she said and without any further ado she blurted out her sorry tale about her failed engagement. Claire was in no state to note Josh's expression, but she just remembered him listening to her patiently, gently stroking her arm and holding her hands as she talked.

After dinner, they took a long walk back to her hotel stopping now and then when they saw some interesting window displays along the way. When they reached Rockefeller Center, Claire felt as though the last drop of alcohol in her body had already evaporated. She asked Josh if she had said anything awkward at dinner.

'No, you didn't. Even at your most inebriated, you'd never say or do anything embarrassing,' Josh said.

'Did I say anything that I would regret?' she asked.

'I hope not. And I wouldn't allow you take back any of your statements anyway.'

'What do you mean?'

'Claire you declared your love for me so eloquently I almost fell on my knees and wept,' he grinned.

'Seriously.'

'You said you love me back and I hope that has not changed yet. It's only been two hours since.'

'That I had said even before my first drink, I think,' she said.

'What do you mean by *that*?' Josh asked.

'That I love you,' she said.

'What? Say that again?' Josh asked.

'That I love you,' Claire said it louder this time although she knew Josh had heard it the first time. 'But I'm also sleepy now, it's almost one and I have yet to finish my packing.'

'Okay, ma'am. We're heading back to your hotel pronto,' Josh said.

She did not remember any more whether Josh had said he loved her before or after her revelation. Perhaps it was Josh's declaration that encouraged her to disclose her history. Or the alcohol. She remembered his saying he loved her more for having made the right decision about her failed engagement.

#

At the airport the next day, Claire dreaded going into immigration. She hugged Josh tightly and would not let go if not for another passenger who needed to pass by with his laden luggage trolley.

'Okay, you better go in now before this guy tells us to get a room,' Josh said.

'I don't want to go,' she tried to stall.

'I'd be the happiest guy on this planet if you'd stay back,' he said.

'Why couldn't you go with me?' she asked.

'I would have loved to if not for this meeting with the studio tomorrow. But I'll catch the first plane to Singapore the first chance I get,' he said stroking her hair gently. 'Now, you must go in or you'll miss the flight,' he kissed her once more.

Claire reluctantly headed to the immigration. She turned and waved at Josh who said he would remain at his spot until after she had boarded her flight. She had been travelling for as long as she could remember and had been going from and arriving at random airports around the world, but she had never felt so heavy-hearted until now. As soon as she reached the airline lounge, she rushed to the washroom and sprayed her face with water, washing off traces of tears.

Claire's return flight was one of the longest routes she had taken, prolonging her emotionally muddled state of mind. She was elated knowing there was someone who loved her genuinely despite all her scars and her family's skeletons. But at the same time, she was on the verge of crying now when it dawned on her that she was already away from Josh so soon after they had just gotten together. Claire had never experienced this emotion in the past. She did not remember feeling this way with Jason. With Josh she was giddy like a teenaged girl that she had to remind herself that she was in her early thirties and had to act appropriately.

Claire could not help but play back the times spent with Josh, the places they had visited: the five different cafés, the three bookshops, and the two theatres. She kept on replaying his dialogues, his puns, and his mannerisms. She was so preoccupied with Josh that she did not even remember to call Melanie and her family before she left New York.

20

Singapore

A long-distance relationship has its ups and downs. The periods of togetherness are marked with intense bonding, but the long stretches of separation in between can put a couple's commitment to the test. While Claire and Josh used technology to be in touch regularly, both were not the type who could tolerate long stretches of physical separation. One month after they had met in New York, Josh came for a quick visit to Singapore.

On this visit, Claire decided to show more of Singapore to Josh who remained impressed with its diversity and cleanliness. Claire took him to the Arab District, starting off at the wall-art covered bar along Haji Lane. After this, they strolled leisurely, stopping now and then to watch artists and musicians who were jamming along the streets. Josh took photos of more wall-arts and colourful doors. They also checked out an ice cream stall in Bussorah Street, which seemed popular among the younger set gauging by the long queue outside. Josh could not resist but join the queue and this was when Claire was more than convinced that he was indeed a huge foodie and always eager to try new things. He came out with two cones of macadamia and *gula melaka*, reversing the order of their meal, as now they were having dessert before dinner. They stood there with their ice cream, contentedly watching passers-by. 'Ah *gula melaka* is the bomb. What is it by the way?' Josh asked belatedly.

'It's some kind of palm sugar,' Claire said.

'Oh man, no wonder! Totally sinful,' Josh smacked his lips exaggeratedly after the last spoonful. 'Even more unforgettable than what we had in Amsterdam,' he said.

In the background, the waxing moon was rising and soon Claire could see it above the golden dome of the Sultan temple. She told Josh about her fascination with the moon and how she had taken so many photos of the different phases of the moon.

'I'd love to see your photos when we get home. Do you know that I'm "lunatic" as well, or has Marc already told you that?' he said.

'What do you mean?' Claire was intrigued.

'I'm a moon fanatic. I collect poems about the moon,' he revealed.

'That's a strange hobby,' she said.

'I'm strange. Haven't you noticed yet?' he teasingly rolled his eyes.

'And what's your favourite moon poem, moon man?' she asked.

'Have you heard of Paul Verlaine?'

'No way,' Claire was suddenly feeling spooked out.

'Yes way,' he said and went on to recite the poem in French. 'So, you see, I had an inkling of where you got your name from,' he smiled.

'It is from that only,' Claire went on to explain.

'What a coincidence, huh. So, have I impressed you enough?'

'Are you sure Marc didn't tell you all this?' she could not believe in so much coincidence.

'Are you sure Marc is even aware of the connection?' he asked, starting to get a bit irritated at Claire's disbelief.

'Fair enough. Sorry,' she said meekly.

They resumed their walk until Kandahar Street. Josh pronounced it their destination upon seeing a nondescript Italian restaurant that, according to him, was known for its gnocchi, lasagna, and cacio e pepe.

'It's all heavy carbs,' Claire complained.

'I didn't know you were watching your weight,' Josh said.

'No, I don't. But I prefer variety in my diet.'

'We'll try their tiramisu then. And their panna cotta. And their cassata,' he pointed at the items on the menu.

'Josh.' Claire said in a serious voice.

'Okay, fine. I know you'll anyways order just one thing. Yes, it's what they really are known for. Your *burrata*,' he smiled.

#

Claire nearly lost Josh in one of the halls of the Buddha Tooth Relic Temple in China Town as he was so intent in reading the names of the Buddha statues that lined the temple walls. When she finally found him, she dragged him towards the Maxwell Hawker Centre. They checked all the stalls before deciding to go back for the chicken rice that had been highly recommended by their taxi uncle that morning. Carrying the chicken rice tray, Josh ushered Claire to an empty table. 'Look, they even have free tissue packets on the table,' he said.

'That means the table is *choped*,' Claire laughed.

'Huh?'

'It's reserved by other customers, so we can't take it,' she explained.

They finally found one without any 'choped' items, on the outer part of the hawker centre, which turned out to be better as it was breezier, and it looked out on to a small garden next to an office building. Josh went back for more food items including the soya bean curd that was Claire's favourite. When an old man in his singlet and rubber slippers came to clear their plates, Josh could not help but say, 'Thank you, uncle,' profusely, which drew a smile from the uncle who was gamely pointing at the high stack of plates from their table alone.

On one weekday night, Claire left the office earlier and met Josh for their Little India excursion. They started off at Mustafa Centre simply to look at the variety of goods, from chocolates and sweets, garments, electronics, to rare spices. They even explored the jewellery floor, and though Josh did not buy anything from this section, he was definitely floored, as he had not seen so much gold in one location before. After this, they crossed over to the Sri Perumal Temple, one of the oldest in Singapore. As what happened in an earlier temple visit, Josh was once more lost in admiration of the intricate architecture. Although this temple was not massive, the detail on the hundreds of sculptures of gods and deities was truly elaborate.

'So now we've ticked off another heritage area,' Claire said on their way out.

'No, not yet,' Josh replied.

'Huh, why?'

'You're missing the most important aspect. My gut instinct tells me that there's an interesting area out here,' he said, as he followed a small map to Race Course Road.

'Silly me. Yes, of course. Come, I'll take you to where they serve the best samosas and biryani in town,' she said. They passed by a row of restaurants and stopped at one with an intricate wooden signage. Claire promptly ordered the two dishes as soon as they were ushered to their table.

'This is by far the hottest food I've ever tried,' Josh said, after biting into the first samosa and immediately drinking two glasses of water afterwards.

'Hotter than jalapeños?' she asked.

'Yep. This is like ten out of ten while jalapeños are probably around eight,' he replied. 'Having said that, I'll definitely try more,' he smiled. 'Now, let's dig into the highly anticipated mutton biryani,' he said, by now sweating and his cheeks somewhat flushed.

#

While Claire was not as enthusiastic as Josh when it came to food, she was glad to share his passion for coffee. Based on his so-called 'desk-research', Josh came up with a list of ten up-and-coming coffee shops that he wanted to check out, a mission that took them to the extreme East Coast and West Coast as well as to Frankel Avenue and the Tiong Bahru estate. The culinary and coffee excursions truly excited Josh, but even Claire, who had been living in Singapore for five years now, relished the discovery of new things.

To prevent weight gain from all their 'taste testing', Claire forced Josh to get up early each day for a run. He was not a big fan of running outdoors, preferring to do his routine in the coolness and comfort of the gym, but he eventually gave in to Claire's nagging and on the third day he even got up a few minutes before Claire's alarm went off. They would run from a section of East Coast Park all the way to the Marina Barrage to catch sunrise. Then they would walk back leisurely, stopping now and then to check out the flora and fauna along the way. Their favourite stop was a pond where Claire watched a mother and baby turtle pair that routinely swam out of the waters and played on the grass patch. Josh even named these two creatures Bella and Ninja. Each morning, Josh would take out breadcrumbs from his pocket to feed the turtles and fishes. One day, a family of otters, crossing the road, on their way to hopping into the next pond, startled Claire and Josh from their feeding session.

'This is totally otter-worldly,' Josh hollered and Claire could not help but laugh at this pun.

The park security cautioned them not to go near the otters and so Josh and Claire contented themselves with watching the romp from a safe distance.

#

Claire felt as though the week had barely started, but in reality, it was now about to be over. She wished she could stretch her timescale and prolong this week in particular. On Josh's last day in Singapore, he decided to cook lunch for Claire. 'Why would you cook on your last day? I'd rather you spend your precious hours with me,' Claire was a bit surprised.

'Just sit back, relax, and watch the Master Chef prepare your favourite dishes,' he said, as he buckled down to work.

'I just find it weird that you're doing it now when you don't have much time.'

'It won't take long. I'll just prepare a bit more than usual and will keep some in the fridge so you don't have to think of what to eat over the next few days,' he explained, taking out the pasta from the cupboard and chicken and herbs from the refrigerator.

'You're just like my mum, always cooking up a storm on the last day of her visit,' she said.

'Now, please don't psychoanalyse. Just read to me while I cook, or better yet, why don't you help me peel these,' he said, handing her a few pieces of onions.

'Then you will literally make me cry,' she chuckled.

'I won't have your tears any other way,' he laughed.

Claire made coffee after lunch and simply clung to Josh and savoured these quiet moments with him. It was a bittersweet day yet again knowing they would be apart for many weeks. She could feel her chest becoming heavier with each minute that passed and as the hour hand moved closer to four o'clock. When his phone alarm went off, Josh insisted on going to the airport on his own so that Claire could rest before her hectic workweek. Soon the cab arrived and they both rushed downstairs for yet another episode of separation.

#

Tagaytay

After their quality time together, it became more difficult for Claire to adjust to the distance from Josh. This, too, coupled with Marc's absence. Her restlessness became magnified whenever she was alone at home. Since meeting Josh, she had forgotten how to be peacefully alone. Now there was this part of her that longed for his presence every time she was alone.

Periods of solitude and longing made Claire realize how detached she could be at times especially when swallowed by her work. Now that she had downtime at work, she decided to call her parents and close relatives, Mimi, and JM, more often. She also carved out more time with her parents who had agreed to meet her in Manila whenever she had time off or a long weekend to spare. This weekend was one of those and her parents picked her up from the airport early in the morning before driving up to Tagaytay for Dino's get-together with friends and fellow organic farmers. After the meet-and-greet at Taal Vista Hotel, Dino joined his friends for a visit to a nearby farm while Claire took Anna to nearby shops that sold artisanal produces and accessories made from indigenous products.

'This is amazing. We can do the same at Buena Vista,' Anna started getting excited with the idea.

'For sure. Jams and preserves go very well with bakery products,' Claire encouraged.

'I'll ask the ladies to start making them in the upcoming harvest season. This should reduce wastage too. Sometimes fruits and vegetables rot unnecessarily because we don't know how to preserve,' Anna said.

'Great idea, Ma. Wait until I've shown you an amazing coffee shop down the road,' Claire said, as they walked to a roadside café, which also sold gourmet coffee beans. They chose a table at the back of the property that looked out over the lake and at the volcano beyond.

'This smells good. I love this coffee,' Anna said after a couple of sips. 'I'm not a coffee person like you, but this is not too bitter nor too bland. I would say it's just right.'

'They grow their own beans. I think their farm is not too far from here,' Claire shared.

'Should we ask if they deliver all the way to Valle Viejo? Maybe I can order some coffee beans from them,' Anna mused.

Claire asked the waitress if they could speak with the proprietor. She returned with another lady who was wearing a sky-blue tunic and white linen pants. She introduced herself as Lydia, a retired nurse who used to live in London. Anna requested if Lydia could join them and Lydia graciously sat on the next chair. Lydia started sharing how she gradually expanded the coffee farm that she inherited from her parents. When it came time to retire, she decided to come back home and set up her dream café.

'I also have a small bakery and coffee shop back home,' Anna started. 'I'd like to check if you could deliver all the way to Valle Viejo.'

Claire thought that Anna was characteristically being humble when she called the shop small. It might have been small when it started, but over a short period of time the bakery and coffee shop, which now operated like a cooperative for the farmer's wives, had expanded. They had added a couple of branches in San Fernando. Claire had started to regard Anna in yet another light. She began to appreciate Anna's affinity to natural products, her innate environment-friendliness, and her nourishing side. She saw Anna's bakery as an embodiment of the many things she stood for, rather than just a fleeting interest.

'Yes, we do. We have a couple of customers and hotel-owners there to whom we deliver once a month,' Lydia smiled warmly.

Claire excused herself to go look at the orchids that bloomed on driftwoods. She took a few photos with her camera phone. When she returned, she was pleasantly surprised that the two ladies were still chatting and laughing at some joke or another. The two exchanged numbers, promising they would catch up again even if only on the phone.

That night Claire and her parents attended the organic farmers' gala at Taal Vista Hotel. 'Daddy, I didn't know you have such a big tribe,' Claire whispered to Dino, seeing the crowded ballroom.

'Of course, *hija*. And this is just the Luzon group. Imagine if it were a national convention,' Dino smiled proudly.

'What's for dinner?' Claire picked up the fancy menu card from the centre of the table.

'Organic food, what else,' Dino replied with one of his rare quips.

A small programme followed after dinner, which Claire decided to skip, opting for a walk around the resort and a quiet time in the courtyard. She ordered a cucumber drink spiked with margarita and was soaking in the cool, but not chilly, air in the courtyard café. She was glad to have carved out time for her family. Claire remembered her grandmother who used to say: 'blood is thicker than water' or 'call of the blood'. For her, family was Dino and Anna, who had built their lives around Claire. Family was Mimi who would rush to her with just one call. Family was JM and Mike who were ready to punch bastards out of her life. Claire felt that blood curdle when it was not nourished. A family could not thrive on blood alone.

Claire thought of Melanie and how she had not revealed the truth about Claire to her parents yet. Melanie was concerned about what the news would do to her parents given their age and attendant fragility. Claire now thought of Melanie as a pendulum. Earlier Melanie seemed to have genuinely cared, especially when she had learned that Claire had had an accident. On the other hand, Melanie's concealing of Claire's existence bordered on cowardice rather than sensitivity to her parents' fragile state. But then again, Melanie made the most difficult effort of introducing Claire to Nate and Melissa. Sometimes Claire did not know where she stood with Melanie.

21

Silicon Valley

Josh visited Claire in San Francisco where Claire was attending a work conference. He resumed his tourist guide act from back in New York the minute he saw Claire. 'For you, mademoiselle, I flew all the way from the East Coast just to show you the beauty of the West,' he grinned.

'I've been here a few times, so I know my way around,' she smiled.

'Ah, and that's how many love stories didn't get to see the light of day, folks. Imagine if I had taken you at your word back in New York. Where would that have left *us*?' he said in mock annoyance.

Despite her protests, Claire quietly admitted that she saw San Francisco with a new lens, through Josh's eyes. They chose destinations that were off the beaten track as well as the Yoda Fountain, the Book Club of California, and City Lights. Josh also took her to an outlet shop, clearly not his favourite part, but he nonetheless indulged Claire knowing that the prices of clothes and accessories here were a lot more reasonable than in Singapore.

Before the visit became filled solely with sightseeing and shopping, Josh reminded her that they should visit his parents who were living in Monterey. Claire agreed to this cheerfully at first, but closer to the date she started to feel anxious.

'Josh, could we please make a U-turn and go back to San Francisco?' she asked half-jokingly on the drive to Monterey the next day.

'Oh please, Louise Parker Junior. You will soon find out that my dad is the nicest dentist you'll ever meet,' Josh glanced at her briefly to note her reaction at his joke before returning his gaze to the highway.

'I know it's not fair, but a dental profession really has a lot of baggage. I hope your mum is not in the same profession?' she asked.

'She's retired from the postal office and is now helping Dad with his books and accounts. Well, I don't know if *help* is the right word. That's what she claims to be doing when she's not busy with her church activities,' he replied.

They passed by Carmel Mission, and drove through narrow but scenic streets. A few minutes later, they entered a leafy neighbourhood. After a few blocks they reached a Spanish colonial set farther away from the road. The front door opened even before Josh could reach the driveway and out came his parents with open arms and warm smiles.

'Dad, Mum, this is Claire. Please don't embarrass me in front of her,' Josh said. 'Claire, this is my Dad, Robert and my Mum, zee Marilynne,' he bowed exaggeratedly.

'Why would we embarrass you in front of the first girl you've ever invited home, Josh?' Robert said with a wide grin.

'Dad, that's already revealing too much,' Josh pretended to protest.

'Oops, I'm sorry, son. Me and my big mouth,' Robert said, patting Josh on the shoulder before turning to Claire. 'We're delighted to finally meet you, Claire. We know how precious you are, especially to our dear Josh,' Robert said more seriously.

'I've heard so much about you . . . from Marc initially and now from Josh, too. And Josh's dad wasn't kidding when he said you are the first girl Josh has invited home. It's a big deal to Josh,' Marilynne started as they settled in the drawing room while Josh and Robert went to the kitchen to prepare the drinks.

'I hope I'm not causing too much inconvenience coming at such a short notice and all,' Claire said. She felt somewhat overwhelmed the more she realized how much this meeting meant to Josh.

'Please don't say that, Claire,' Marilynne replied. She was a Filipina who had migrated with her parents to the United States in the early sixties. While retired from the workforce, Marilynne did not look her age. She had a short, but well-styled, bob and had smooth, supple skin. She was slim and moved around with determined efficiency. She was in a light-blue top under a long, white cardigan that reached down to the knees of her fitted tan slacks. She wore a thin white gold necklace with a dainty cross pendant. 'We love having my sons' friends over, and since you are a great friend of Marc, and more importantly, since you are very special to Josh, all the more reason to have you,' she smiled.

'Marilynne, darling, where do you keep the glasses for white wine?' Robert called from the kitchen.

'Dear Lord, these men. They'd rather use their mouths than their eyes,' Marilynne rolled her eyes before answering, 'They're in the rightmost cupboard, labelled "glasses", honey.' When it seemed to be taking them longer than expected, Marilynne called, 'Josh, please come here, honey, so I can help your dad fix the drinks. It might take forever if we leave it all to him.'

'What is Josh doing, wasn't he supposed to help his dad?' Claire was curious.

'Knowing him, he's probably just sitting there, watching his dad agonize,' she replied.

'I heard that Mum, and NO, I'm not totally useless,' Josh emerged from the kitchen proudly carrying a wooden cheeseboard filled with thinly sliced ham, sausages, and three different varieties of cheese.

'Josh, I prepared that earlier. I'm sure you just picked that up from the counter,' Marilynne said, before going into the kitchen to help her husband.

'What do you have in there?' Claire asked, typically not curious about food, but since Josh's mum had prepared this, she suddenly wanted to know what went into it.

'It has your favourite cheese, at least,' he said, pointing to the brie and camembert. He sliced a piece of the cheese, spread it on the table cracker and fed it to Claire.

'Josh, please don't embarrass me,' she said, quickly eating the cracker and hurriedly brushing the crumbs from her lips.

'Welcome to Casa Serra, where you can be yourself without fear of being judged,' he said, as he ate a slice of ibérico ham.

'Mum, Claire loves the cheese,' he said, as his parents walked in.

'I'm glad you do. I bought it from the Sunday farmers' market,' Marilynne smiled as she handed Claire's wine.

'Dad, isn't too much cheese bad for the teeth? Isn't it calcium on calcium?' he asked.

'The teeth are not made of calcium, Josh. But they need calcium to remain strong, you should have remembered that,' Robert chided him. 'Welcome to our mad house, young lady,' he said, raising his glass to hers.

'Thank you so much for the warm welcome,' Claire replied.

'Don't be too formal with us, Claire,' Marilynne said sitting next to her on the deep tan, leather sofa.

'Yes, Claire, don't be intimidated by dad's height and serious countenance,' Josh added.

'Josh, remember that I still have some blackmail materials in my drawer,' Robert said, raising an eyebrow at Josh.

'No, Daddy, no.' Josh replied, pretending to be a traumatized child, clearly in his full comic element.

'Please ignore these guys. They're like kids despite their age,' Marilynne said.

Both Robert and Marilynne loved their routine here, gardening in their yard, walking to the beach in the mornings, and being actively involved in their community. Robert could not live a week without playing golf at Pebble Beach. Marilynne had her circles from the church and her ex-colleagues.

'Yes, there's more to Monterey than Cannery Row,' Robert said towards the end of the three-hour lunch, filled with tales of Monterey.

'Or the Aquarium. I'm glad I found that out on this trip,' Claire said. To her any place with a great view of the ocean was paradise. While Monterey had that too, it was a lot more charming than she had thought.

'I'll take you around a bit more on the way back,' Josh told her.

'Take her to the lone cypress tree,' Marilynne suggested.

Robert invited Claire to stay over, but Claire declined politely as she did not have much time. 'Josh, please convince Claire to stay longer next time,' Robert added.

'Of course, Dad, I will. Shall I book her next dental appointment then?' he joked.

Before dessert, Marc called via FaceTime. 'This is so unfair. Why are you guys getting together without me,' he said.

Josh naturally made him more jealous by showing off the 'feast' that Marilynne had prepared, including the luscious peach-topped panna cotta that Claire could not wait to dig into. Claire was flattered that Marilynne had prepared a dessert that she genuinely liked. She looked at Josh who simply shrugged, pretending it was a coincidence. After dessert, Marilynne offered to show her around the house while Josh and Robert cleared the table and did the dishes. The house was fairly large with two bedrooms on the ground floor and three larger rooms on the first floor, including the master bedroom with its cosy balcony. Josh and Marc's rooms were adjacent to their parents' room. Marilynne even showed her stacks of Marvel, and other comics that Josh had kept since childhood. Claire admired how Josh's parents managed to hold on to these memorabilia without making the rooms feel as if they were museums. They were neatly tucked in and arranged chronologically on the cabinet that lined one side of the room. 'Wow, these comics could be worth a fortune on eBay. They are vintage,' Claire said, while checking the spines and seeing issues from as far back as the early eighties when each had cost only a dollar.

'I've been telling him to dispose of these things or I'll start charging him storage fee already, but no, he simply clings to them,' Marilynne said.

'You guys were generous with his allowance,' she noted.

'No, we were never generous with cash when they were kids. He earned that himself, either by mowing the neighbours' lawns or running errands for me and his dad,' Marilynne explained.

'No wonder he does not want to part with them. They are proof of his hard work,' she smiled.

#

Josh picked up Claire from Mimi's place where she was staying during her last few days in the city. They drove down to a charming vineyard in Napa Valley where they had wine and cheese tasting. When it was time for lunch, they moved to the glass porch of the restaurant that looked out to the vast orchard and the scenic Vaca Mountains in the backdrop. Claire could have sat here all day. She was almost oblivious to the carefully presented food, as she soaked in this serene panorama before her. Josh even waved to bring her attention back to their conversation.

'Since you weren't listening, I've made a unilateral decision and ordered our dessert,' he said. That got her attention and Claire now looked at him with surprise because she did not have a sweet tooth and except for ice cream, she typically skipped dessert in favour of coffee. When the waiter came, he served a small white cake that Josh said was for them to share. He asked her to slice the cake. She carefully removed the fresh rosebuds on top. There were three of them, each in pink, red, and orange, surrounded by tiny button flowers. She started slicing the cake and was puzzled by the cake's hard core. Josh had to help her and that was how she discovered the small box inside.

'Don't just stare at it. Please open it,' Josh asked.

'Josh, I seriously am not expecting this,' she said, as she hesitantly opened the tiny box. Claire was almost speechless as she took the ring from its case. She handed it to him and watched him put it gently on her finger, her face reflecting mixed emotions, alternating between smiling and frowning.

'You're supposed to be ecstatic, jumping with joy and shouting a big "YES" all over the place,' Josh was sombre all of a sudden.

'There's nothing I want more. But I'm also feeling overwhelmed and scared,' she said.

'Scared is the last reaction I expected from you,' Josh was taken aback.

'Look, honey, I'm a bit surprised and seriously wasn't expecting it at this stage,' Claire sighed.

'There's nothing impulsive about this from my end. When I made this decision, it was not something I randomly came up with after a toss of a coin,' he said.

'I know, Josh. And I wish this came at a better time when I could match your enthusiasm. With all that has happened to me lately, I don't know if I can give justice to this proposal,' she said, biting her bottom lip.

'I wish you could set the other issues aside. Stop dwelling on the past, and start celebrating the two of us,' he said solemnly.

'I'm sorry,' she said, leaning over to hug him. 'But, yes, I do want to live the rest of my life with you, only with you,' she added almost in a whisper.

'I will wait for the time when you can say that with a happy face. Only with a happy face. Then we can talk again,' he said simply. 'In all my thirty-five years, I have never thought of proposing to anyone. I've had relationships in the past and ironically, I was the one who ended at least one of them because I did not want to be rushed into marriage.'

Josh was tight-lipped on the drive back and did not even bother to go into Mimi's house with Claire. He just said he'd pick her up the next day for the airport drop-off.

That night, Claire had a long talk with Mimi who helped her flesh things out. But she could not sleep even after the chat. She kept on berating herself for her stupidity and selfishness. At dawn, she called Josh and begged him to come earlier so that they could have more time together before her flight.

'I'm sorry, I was being selfish,' she said, the minute she opened the door to Josh.

'I had a feeling you would not be able to sleep,' he said, hugging her and kissing her forehead. 'I was tempted to call you at midnight, but I thought I'd give you your space, so you could think things through properly,' he replied.

Mimi also got up early and led them to the round table in the eat-in kitchen before quickly making coffee and heating bagels and muffins.

Claire gathered all the happy thoughts she could muster, held Josh's hand, smiled at him and said, 'And here's my big Ye . . . eee . . . ees!'

'Congratulations, Josh. I'm so excited for you and Claire,' Mimi said, hugging Josh.

'Thanks, Auntie Mimi,' he said enthusiastically. He looked at Claire, lifted her chin and kissed her on the forehead, then on the lips before embracing her tightly. 'You should have told me to invite Auntie Mimi along yesterday. I didn't realize you needed her by your side for you to be able to say yes with greater conviction,' he could now tease Claire about the situation. 'Okay, before we make a move, let's quickly call the parents, yours and mine. I want them to hear it from us, first.' Josh said.

22

Tagaytay

Claire felt strangely calm on her wedding day. She did not feel any jitters, as some brides were supposedly wont to feel. The pseudo-psychoanalyst in her thought that perhaps this was a kind of defence mechanism against any potential slip-up.

But the same could not be said about the father of the bride. On the ride to the church, Dino was visibly overwhelmed. 'I can't explain how happy I am to see you like this,' he said.

'Daddy, you make me feel as if you're relieved that I won't remain a spinster after all,' she said, reaching out to hold Dino's hand.

'You don't know how much I want to see you with your own family. And I can't wait to start playing with my grandchildren. I hope I can do this before I become too senile,' he said.

Anna gently dabbed the corners of her eyes. 'Dino, please stop the drama now. Claire and I are wearing make-up. I don't want any smudges before the family photos are taken,' Anna said. Claire knew that Anna was serious about the smudges.

Seeing Dino and Anna in moments of happiness like this reaffirmed Claire's decision to have this church wedding in the Philippines and let her parents regale in the role they rightfully deserved.

Claire and Josh wanted a small wedding with only the immediate family and close friends. But Dino and Anna wanted to have an elaborate one in Santa Rosa. Claire did not have any sentimental attachment to her hometown now, having been away much longer than she had actually lived in there. Besides, she did not want her most important day to become a spectacle, like the political sorties of the past. Ultimately, they reached a compromise and chose an intimate chapel in Tagaytay. A garden reception would follow, and they had likewise invited just a small contingent for this.

#

Soon the white Mercedes Benz bridal limousine stopped in front of the church. From the car, Claire could see Marc and Pia waving at her, and both were literally leaping up and down in excitement to get her attention. She waved to her family and friends who were part of the entourage. Soon the wedding coordinator came over to inform her that they were all set. Pia straightened Claire's gown while they were waiting on the church's steps. JM and Mike hugged her tight and Claire, pretending to be a toughie, declared there should not be any more tears from anyone else as she could see that JM's eyes were starting to glisten. Claire could now hear the church orchestra playing the first few notes of Pachelbel's *Canon in D Major*. Before the church door opened, Claire hugged her parents once more. She could feel both of them taking deep breaths. She quickly squeezed both their arms and with that they smiled and marched to the door and were welcomed by the warm applause of their family and friends who were waiting inside the church.

Claire felt as though she was gliding, perhaps because Dino and Anna seemed to carry her through the aisle and partly because the three of them were all buoyed by the good cheers. Mimi and Paul led the sponsors. JM, Mike and their families all had special roles in the entourage. Marc and Pia exceeded Claire's expectation in their roles of best man and bridesmaid respectively. They would have been perfect except for the funny faces they made at her on her way to the altar. And there, waiting near the altar and visibly nervous, was Josh, with his beaming parents.

#

That Claire's wedding turned out to be the occasion she had wished for was partly due to the absence of some characters in her life. Ric, for one, was not in any condition to attend the wedding. It never occurred to Claire to invite him initially but she gave in to Dino and Mimi's insistence and so she eventually did, although grudgingly. On the wedding day, though, Ric was at one of his hospital confinements yet again because of his chronic kidney disease that required him to go for dialysis more frequently now. He, however, called Claire and Josh the day before to wish them well. Claire recognized this as a sign of softening from Ric's side, though she knew that she would never feel any affection for Ric.

As for Melanie, she had taken Claire to Alexander McQueen's Savage Beauty exhibit at The Met on her most recent trip to New York. During a break at the museum coffee shop, Claire had asked if she and Frank would be able to come to the wedding.

Melanie had hesitated before answering her.

'It's okay. You don't have to answer me right now. I understand that you want to give it more thought,' Claire had said.

'It's a bit complicated. Frank and I would love to go under any other circumstance. But the more I'd thought about it, the more I realized that my mere presence there could only distract from your most important day,' she had said.

'I've also thought about that, but I don't really care much about what other people think. Besides, we're inviting just family and our closest friends. It's not going to be a society wedding.'

'I'm glad that it's going to be a more intimate celebration. It makes it more solemn and meaningful that way,' Melanie had paused. 'The other reason for my hesitation, and I hope you'll be with me on this one, is that I don't want to take away from your parents on that day. It's their day. As much as I would like to see you on that important day, they deserve to have that moment with you,' she had said sadly.

'I know. Just thinking of them makes me feel so emotional now,' she remembered saying.

'My only request now is if I could give you a small reception here in New York after the wedding. You can invite Marc and Steve of course, and Josh's parents,' Melanie had said.

#

At the garden reception after the wedding ceremony, Claire held Josh's hands as she soaked in the glow of the day. They were sitting together listening to family and friends as they entertained them with toasts and singing and slideshows. Claire looked again at Dino and Anna, who were now sharing a good laugh with Robert and Marilynne at the nearby table. She could not help but look up and be truly grateful for this day.

23

Santa Rosa, Valle Viejo

For a long time, Claire had not visited and did not want to visit Valle Viejo to avoid the curiosity from the spectacle that befell her clan after the separation of Ric and Cecille years ago. On her more recent visits to the Philippines she had asked Dino and Anna to meet her in Manila and later, when she could not travel as often, she had requested her parents and close relatives to visit her in Singapore instead.

It was yet another election season and with pressure from JM, Claire decided to go for a visit this time. She noticed the many changes since her last visit five years ago. New fast-food chains and malls lined Valle Viejo's main roads. She heard from her cousins that there were more graduates from bigger cities who had gone back to the province to set up small businesses. Their entrepreneurial imprint could be seen in the new cafés every few miles or so. There were new establishments not seen before in the province including a world-class amusement park, a newly opened zoo, and a reopened national park.

There had been concerted efforts to revitalize the capital city of San Fernando. A couple of old mansions, similar to the Rosales's, were converted to bed-and-breakfasts, while another was converted into a heritage museum that housed old furniture, household and farming implements, and many memorabilia from the Spanish colonial era. Three private schools, including a real Montessori, with higher quality standards opened in San Fernando. She could also see signs of gentrification as they passed by the suburbs, starting with the up-and-coming cafés and restaurants around the big cathedral in the outskirts of the city.

As the car drew closer to Santa Rosa, Claire started to see similar signs of progress in her hometown, albeit at a smaller scale. New houses had sprung up in erstwhile empty lots, some reflecting architectural influences from North America and Europe. The driver saw how curious she was and filled her in on the latest. In the Rosales's district alone, there were at least four families that had returned from London for retirement. It was unimaginable before but now there was an owner and operator of a thriving bus line in their own town courtesy of a British retiree. One of the new houses even had a swimming pool, almost unheard of in Santa Rosa before. The overall spirit was far more upbeat than what she remembered.

The Rosales House itself seemed the only place that had not undergone any major changes. It remained grand from the outside, with its off-white walls and its clay tile roof gleaming in the sun. But as she entered her grandmother's home, Claire knew that only the exterior remained unchanged. Inside, the house looked dimmer, partly because of the darker curtains. Claire also noticed that the Amorsolo painting that used to grace the drawing room was no longer there as with two other prominent pieces from Manansala and Ang Kiukok. They were replaced by darker-toned abstract paintings that did not go well with the classic interior. The long-time staffers were still there but similarly, she thought, they looked different. For one Maritess had more grey hair and the wrinkles on her forehead more visible.

This time around, the election battle was also different as Ric was no longer part of it. He had fully quit politics and was now living with his second family in Manila. Claire knew that this was not entirely due to her threat but was more due to a confluence of other factors including his deteriorating health. After a kidney transplant that had allowed him a few healthy years, Ric had a relapse and was again spending more time in the hospital. Claire was relieved she did not have to do an exposé on Ric, though, she was prepared to carry out her earlier threat had the situation called for it. She was grateful her clan was spared any more drama.

'I'm so relieved that you're here,' JM hugged her tightly as soon as she entered the war-room. 'I can never thank you enough for this.'

'Oh please, don't make it sound as though it were a huge favour. It's my duty, too, to help in rebuilding our image,' Claire repeated JM's earlier words.

It was not a question of whether Claire had to come or not for this round of election. It was her duty to be there for JM who was running for congress and trying to reclaim the position that Ric had lost three years ago. It was up to the younger generation to reclaim the Rosales's heritage.

Claire pored over the results of the latest survey and was confident that JM had a big chance of winning. While Fernandez, the opponent, won by a tiny margin in the last election, the electorate was not happy with his performance in the past three years. Apparently, he mismanaged the funds for farm-to-market roads intended to ease farmers' travel. He was also nowhere to be seen when the strongest typhoon in recent memory hit Valle Viejo and left thousands of villagers homeless. These were some of the ills that Claire heard from the group discussions that she had attended. 'You have a good chance, JM. This ten-point advantage is statistically significant. If the election were held today, you would have a clear lead,' Claire read the results out to the family members who were in attendance in the war-room.

'I can't afford to be complacent. You know how deceitful the Fernandez camp is. They can easily cheat in the elections. If they are capable of worse things, cheating will not be beneath them,' JM said.

'Then your team needs to mobilize and train your poll-watchers thoroughly. Make sure that we have a representative at every polling place,' Mimi said. 'We are not going to lose any more elections, come what may,' she added, pacing around the war-room.

'Yes Auntie, we have taken that into account,' JM confirmed. 'Mike is working closely with all the volunteer poll-watchers including the core group from Uncle Dino's cooperative. Mummy is also coordinating with the Free Election watchers to make sure we are well covered across precincts,' he added.

Mimi quickly drew a diagram on the whiteboard and listed all the poll-watching groups and the corresponding points of contact from JM's team. When she was assured that all areas were covered, she told the team that they could take a short break for lunch.

JM requested Claire to stay back to clarify some numbers. He was estimating the worst-case scenario votes in areas that were not a Rosales stronghold and reviewing where he could compensate for the potential losses. Claire tallied the figures and pointed out the areas that needed priority in the remaining days.

Claire admired JM's resolve to reclaim the Rosales's lustre after all that had taken place. 'I know that you had entertained the idea of coming back here many years ago, but I never expected you to actually do it,' Claire said.

'It was a tough decision. I could have gradually climbed the career ladder at the bank. While stressful, it was more stable and could have been more financially rewarding in the long run,' he replied.

'My thoughts exactly,' she said.

'I started to seriously consider coming back when Daddy and Mummy separated. The desire intensified when Daddy lost in the last election. That year's Christmas was the bleakest in my memory. There was just my family, Mike's, Mummy, and Auntie Mimi. They all tried to brighten the atmosphere, but their efforts could not make up for everyone else's absence, including your family's,' he sighed at the memory.

JM resigned from his banking job in Hong Kong and moved back three years ago, setting up house at a San Fernando subdivision. He and his wife, Kris, founded a trading company exporting and importing goods from Hong Kong. JM then joined several civic organizations and Ric's political party. He gradually rose through the ranks by actively contributing to the party. Consequently, he managed to get the party's endorsement when he decided to run for congress despite this being his first foray into politics and that this was a recovery effort from the last election. It helped that Cecille's side of the family also had considerable influence, bolstering JM's earlier bid for the party nomination.

'I know that everybody wanted me to patch things up with Uncle Ric and come home back then, but I couldn't bring myself to do that. I had known then, from the survey results, that he was losing, and I thought that was justice enough,' she explained.

'It wasn't your fault. I had also blamed Daddy a lot, but later I realized I should stop because constant blaming would lead us nowhere.'

'I love you and Mike a lot, but you know that I wouldn't have been able to face myself in the mirror if I had pretended to root for Uncle Ric in that last election.'

'It was actually brave of you to have stayed out despite the pressure from us. You stuck to your principles. You were clear about your moral compass.'

'We, each of us, had to fight our battles in the only way that we knew how.'

'Right. In any case, after that Christmas, I decided that I should do my share in bringing back the light to this home. Besides, if I had stayed back in Hong Kong and let the Rosales decline continue, what would I tell Nicole in the future? That we used to be this respected clan, but then it was more convenient to be away than to fight for that legacy? I want her to be proud of our clan, even if much of the pride had to be resurrected,' JM said.

'What did Uncle Ric say about your running for this election?' she asked, more impressed than ever with JM's commitment to the clan.

'I think he underestimated me. It didn't occur to him that I would be running for public office. But then he was too sick to say anything. He couldn't recover after that election loss. In the past, it was Lola who had guided and given him pep-talks at every step,' he said.

'You mean he was a puppet?' Claire was surprised that she did not know this.

'Yes, it was always Lola who had to pull him out. He was like a child that way. He was not capable on his own,' JM said.

She nodded, remembering that her own existence was a testament to Gloria's effort in saving Ric from a big scandal.

'Now I'm officially part of this world despite my earlier reservations. I know what your opinion of politics is and you're not alone in that. I have friends, too, who find it as repulsive as you do. But we have no right to criticize if we haven't done anything to make things better. I'm going in with my eyes open and I'm hoping that I can help to redefine this arena,' he said.

'You're the bravest person I know. I truly admire your courage and dedication. You are our phoenix and I'm extremely proud of you,' Claire said.

'I couldn't have done this without Uncle Dino's and Auntie Mimi's commitment to support me all the way. I also know that both you and Mike will give your all for me. And I wasn't mistaken. You are here now.'

'Oh, it was the least that I could do,' Claire said teary-eyed.

'It's not a small thing. It does a lot for my morale. Your presence here is the strongest indication of our clan's unity. So yes, even if you do not stump in all those sorties, your mere presence here is the message, and people get that. They know that you're in town, that you're here at the Rosales House, and that we're a united and solid clan. You might not be aware of it, but there's always a stronger buzz whenever you're in town. All the helpers get more excited,' JM smiled.

'JM, please, you don't need to flatter me, I'm already here.'

'I'm not humouring you. I'm not the type, as you know. I'm just stating the truth. Never in my life have I been met by Maritess with so much excitement.'

'That's just Maritess.'

'Yes, because the others are too shy to come forward, but you should see them,' JM said.

'Okay, fine. You're making me feel self-conscious now,' Claire said.

'It's ironic isn't it that the most interesting person in the clan is the most elusive one,' he said.

'The most boring, you mean,' she shook her head.

'There's no way I could ever convince you,' he said, hugging her before they stepped out to join the rest of the clan.

24

Buena Vista

On the evening of the election Claire left the war-room to go for a much-needed run. She was feeling antsy now after being cooped up at the Rosales House's library for three consecutive days. Claire ran around Buena Vista's perimeter road, which she noticed was now asphalted all the way to the next province. The breeze was, as she remembered it, fresh with the smell of trees and grasses. She stopped now and then to smell the flowers that escaped from the fences. She smiled at herself upon realizing that she literally stopped to smell the flowers. Ever since she had ticked off her goal of running the New York City marathon three years ago, Claire's attitude towards running had become more relaxed. She still needed to do it regularly to ward off any anxiety build-up. But now she tended to savour her run more, paying greater attention to the things that she passed by, and less on the metrics on her fitness tracker.

After her run, Claire joined Josh and Andrea who were busy exploring the area around the pond. It was their first time to visit Valle Viejo and they took to Buena Vista instantly—their refuge from the chaos at the Rosales House and a better alternative to the extreme quiet at Dino and Anna's house. Andrea enjoyed chasing the geese, turkeys, and other fowls in the farm. From there, Claire took them around to show her four-year-old daughter some of the tallest trees,

'Look at those trees, I planted them many, many moons ago,' she scooped up Andrea to show her a row of three-decade-old trees.

'They are so tall, Mama,' Andrea was in awe of the eucalyptus trees. 'Why are they so far away from the other trees?' she asked.

'You are such a perceptive kiddo. That type of tree releases compounds that are not good for the other plants,' Claire replied.

'Why did you plant it if it is bad?' Andrea asked again.

'This tree, used in the right way, can also heal. So it has its good side too,' Claire explained.

'So it is both good and bad, good and bad. How do you know?' Andrea started her never-ending inquisition.

'When we're back at Lola Anna's house later, I'll show you a book that explains how it works,' Claire said.

'Okay, Mama,' Andrea said, before running off to chase a pair of geese nearby.

'You didn't tell me you have a little paradise in here, honey. We should have visited earlier and could have spent most of our vacations here,' Josh said, resting his hand on her lower back. 'Tagaytay, Boracay and all are nice, but this to me is a personal paradise.'

'There's always a time and a season for everything, as you know. Earlier, when the wound was still fresh, I didn't have the strength to come back.'

'I should thank JM for deciding to run for congress. If not for him, we wouldn't be here, at this exact spot, today,' Josh said, pointing at the soil he was standing on. He lifted her chin and kissed her lips gently.

'Yep, we should definitely thank him,' Claire said. Back in the corporate world, Claire had a straightforward path and was likely to continue climbing the hierarchy. After all, in her field of specialization, consistency was the name of the game. Even Josh had found a rewarding profession, teaching creative writing at a leading arts college in Singapore. They could continue to carve out a comfortable niche for their immediate family. She did not need to revisit the chaos that Santa Rosa represented. But pretending the latter did not exist would be tantamount to erasing her past. While too colourful for her at times, Santa Rosa and Valle Viejo had many gems that she treasured and cared for. She might have been a coward for not leading the next generation of Rosales's out of the difficult situation they were in, but it was not too late yet. And in JM, she had a conduit for rebuilding a legacy that future generations could be proud of. This was her world too. While this world was miles away from her ordinary life, Claire did not need to relinquish it. She could continue to be part of it, just as her Auntie Mimi had been doing all these years.

'Snap out of it, honey. I know by that glazed-eye look that you're lost in your own reverie,' Josh squeezed her shoulders.

'I was just thinking how different things are out here from our everyday lives back in Singapore. Somehow, I still find it hard to reconcile these two different worlds,' she said.

'Honey, we are thousands of years from the caveman era. We can and must adapt to different settings. Besides, if not for your openness to adjust to different situations, would you have met your prince charming?' he grinned at her.

She pretended to roll her eyes. 'Anyways, what have you two been doing while I was out in the battlefield?' Claire looked at Andrea who was now tugging at her tracksuit.

'I was tagging along with either JM or Mike. So yes, I know how to shake hands with the folks the Santa Rosa way,' Josh winked.

'What about this little one?' Claire asked.

'She was with the grandmothers and the cousins. She was busy running around and making sure that the three Lolas get their exercise for the day,' Josh added.

'Doing pretty much the things I did, huh?' she pinched her daughter's cheeks.

'What do you mean, Mama?' Andrea asked.

'Ah, that you are such a lucky girl,' Josh picked her up from Claire and carried her piggyback. They ran towards the house upon seeing that the family van was coming up the driveway. Claire could see her parents and Mimi alighting from the car, with Anna holding a cake box from her bakery. Then another car drove in—it was Cecille with JM's daughter, Nicole, and Mike's three kids. They were not celebrating any birthdays today, but the grandparents had been indulging the kids this season. They clambered to the porch to make balloons and kites, skills that Dino had been teaching them over the past few days. Soon after, two other SUVs arrived. Perhaps her cousins needed some private time away from the mansion too.

Claire followed her family to the house, its paint newly recoated in its original white and green colour combination. It was only six in the evening, but she could already see the crescent moon ascending above the cathedral that was visible from the highest point on the hill. Buena Vista, like the mansion in Santa Rosa, had been with her family for generations. As with other things that had seen generations, it was a witness to the Rosales's peaks and troughs. Years ago, she would never have thought that her clan was strong enough to withstand powerful storms. But as with the farm, where sturdy trees survived the storms that came to pass and conversely, trees that were weak in the core inevitably fell at the slightest gust of wind, the clan might have been weakened but not entirely broken. Some trees might have fallen, but new trees had also sprung up after the storm.

Claire looked at the evening sky. Even the new moon had no ambivalence. It was shining brightly, brighter than the more powerful but distant stars. On this piece of land nestled in the soft fold of the valley, surrounded by trees that stood as a fortress against the outside world, the three generations of Rosaleses gathered together and savoured this respite from the noise of politics. As she approached the winding path to the front steps, Claire could hear even the tiniest sound such as the rustling of leaves when the wind blew this way. She could see the glint of the moon on the tips of budding flowers that lined the cobbled path to the wooden but sturdy farmhouse. For once she did not want to roll out her imaginary time scale; she wanted time to slow down.

Acknowledgments

Writing a book takes a village, and I'm fortunate to have a wonderful one. Thanks to my village people, including:

1. My wonderful early readers: my first beta reader and vision illustrator, Sidney Bravo, who's wise beyond her years; Helen Mangham, for her generosity with her time and invaluable suggestions especially on character development; Baby C for her candid comments on the tone
2. My friends who are also amazing editors: Baby C (again) for her help in editing the first few chapters and for always encouraging me to persevere. Claire Betita de Guzman for helping me with the long synopsis and her feedback on the first few chapters
3. Nora, for her sharp eye in checking for clarity. And most importantly for helping me realize one of my big dreams
4. My *Get Lucky* family and fellow writers in Singapore for their encouragement and all the help
5. Mama and my brothers for all their support, past and present
6. Bubba and Taatu for understanding what it takes to be a writer, and for giving me the space and time to create.